The Resurrected

The Resurrected

Published by The Conrad Press in the United Kingdom 2023

Tel: +44(0)1227 472 874
www.theconradpress.com
info@theconradpress.com

ISBN 978-1-915494-65-8

Typesetting and Cover Design by:
Charlotte Mouncey, www.bookstyle.co.uk

The Conrad Press logo was designed by Maria Priestley.

Printed and bound in Great Britain by Clays Ltd, Elcograf S.p.A.

The Resurrected

A.N. Drew

Chapter One

Doug Spencer lay back in his armchair in front of the log fire, legs outstretched and crossed. Ruby, his rescued golden retriever lay in front of the fire, head between her paws as she looked up at Dad. He seemed genuinely concerned as periodically he sighed deeply. Doug was looking back over the past year, an eventful time that had passed so quickly. What would this year bring? As much as the passing one; no surely not, nothing could surpass that. Or could it...

Tracey was uppermost in his mind. The local journalist from *The Wiltshire Chronicle* who had started their relationship; let him down, getting back together, moving on with their mutual interest in classic cars. But where were they now? Oh, she had been very supportive once they had got their differences sorted out, even during them. He might not have got through his trials and tribulations without her. Yes he would, but having Tracey at his side had felt comfortable, meant to be.

What had happened during the past year - how did it all start? Well he had moved into the little Wiltshire cottage on his retirement from ministry. He shuddered. The unbelievable loneliness of retiring after losing Mary the year before. Dark times, very dark. Brightened by finding his beautiful Ruby at a dog rescue centre on a Tuesday. Ruby Tuesday began his recovery process which gathered speed from that moment. She had been the key that opened so many doors, truly amazing doors. One leading into another, and another, and another. But is there more?

Retired disillusioned Anglican vicar makes good. That would make a headline and a half. He stared into the flames. Fire purifies. But also destroys. Out of ashes something positive can arise...

He should meet with Tracey, take stock. How do you take stock of a relationship? Surely it is or it is not, no in between. He put her to the back of his mind for the moment. He needed to take stock of recent events, explore where he is up to. There are people, there are places, in my life. His life had seemed over when he moved into the cottage alone. Loneliness is a dark, all-consuming cold existence, a place to wallow or rise up from, shake yourself down and welcome new challenges. There had been plenty of those along the way.

Doug took a sip from his favourite coffee mug as he cradled it between his hands. Dreams can become reality but the strange thing was he hadn't had dreams; he had followed a path from one stage to another until arriving at a most unexpected place, one he could never have dreamed of, even in his wildest nightmares.

He looked at Ruby and reflected on how their meeting had

been such an important opening chapter of his adventures. His visit to the dog rescue centre on a cold February morning. Snow falling, her sadness, the way they had seemed to gel in their mutual sorrow. Both had been dumped; Doug through the passing of his wife Mary shortly before his retirement, Ruby through the passing of her previous owner.

He could not have imagined how their adventure together would progress; from a retired Anglican vicar with grave doubts about his past ministry to Pastor Doug, a non-denominational pastor of a growing congregation of needy people. The mobile trailer offering food had developed into more permanent prem-ises in a rented town centre shop, with room for a small chapel.

The people he had encountered on his journey. Thelma and Wally had grown from strength to strength. Doug had met them whilst visiting his father's Ford V8 Pilot classic car; they had introduced him to Pastor Jim who became Doug's mentor and his lonely world had become full of exciting challenges.

He looked at his watch. Nearly seven o'clock, he'd better get ready for the evening session. He had prepared everything during the morning, part of his daily routine.

Ruby stirred, lifted her head and yawned. Tea-time. They went into the kitchen and as Ruby chomped away in her bowl, Doug stared out of the window, thinking about Thelma and Wally. The disadvantaged couple brought up in care who had lived in a derelict caravan near where the Pilot was stored; their move to the rundown town of Maidenbury near his village so they could help with 'The Happening'. That was when things really took off!

It was getting dark and he stared at his reflection in the window. Silvering hair, neatly trimmed with compassionate features surrounded by a greying beard. Not bad for a sixty-seven year old he mused. Tracey had to be thanked for the trimmed hair and beard though. Tracey. Not now Doug, not now...

Long Day's Journey into Night. Yes it had been a long journey, very long, but it had lead into bright sunshine. Meeting Thelma and Wally, then Pastor Jim and others had certainly turned things around. From intense loneliness and a deep feeling of failure. He could have stayed there, wallowed in self-pity, blamed the world, or move on. He was in wonder how events happened, one after another in almost precise order. Was it meant to be? Seemed like it.

Ruby looked up from her empty bowl and began lapping water from her water bowl. Predictable, one followed the other. Doug felt hungry and pulled a dish of stew from the 'fridge, putting it in the microwave. Tasted good last night at the centre, should still be OK now. He poured it into a bowl and sat at the kitchen table with a glass of water as Ruby hovered expectantly.

He waved his spoon at her. 'You've had yours greedy, this is for me, thank you.'

She cocked her head to one side and lay down at his feet. She knew alright but hope springs eternal.

He would see Thelma and Wally shortly, as he did every evening at the centre where food and brief shelter were provided seven days a week for the needy of Maidenbury. Should he ring Tracey and arrange to meet her?

'Well Ruby, you tell me. It's now or never.'

She looked up at him with a puzzled expression. Dad's not happy. What does he want me to do? Doug patted her and gave her a treat.

'I know you didn't like Tracey at first but that changed. You like her now, don't you?'

Ruby stared at him. Well yes and no. She hadn't liked Tracey at first because there was something not quite right. Then Dad got upset, then it got sorted. Now he seems halfway to paradise. Don't worry Dad, I've got your back. Always.

He reflected on their meeting at her house to try to patch up their failing relationship. Tracey had smiled as she poured coffee in the modern lounge.

'Remember when we sat here and drank from mugs?'

Doug had looked up from his bone china cup. 'Yep, sure do. Maybe we're more refined now.'

'Oh, I think we've always been that Doug. In a down to earth sort of way.'

They had drunk in silence. Ruby had peered from between her paws as she lay on the soft warm beige carpet. Their voices sounded calm, friendly even. Everything should be OK.

He had looked round. 'I do like this room Tracey, and the conservatory. In fact the whole house.'

It was a three-bedroom detached on a new estate, a couple of miles the other side of the village from his quaint cottage. Part of the settlement of her divorce from Dave, an architect. They had no children.

Doug had observed her, an attractive brunette in her early fifties. The age difference of fourteen years was not a problem, they enjoyed so many similar interests. Not least a love of classic cars. Tracey's pristine white 1963 MG Midget in the attached double garage was often a talking point. They had driven into the countryside for picnics and she loved driving the Pilot when he took her to the lock-up for visits.

In fact over the past twelve months they had got to know each other well. Very well. 'The Happening' was a make or break event but they had survived. She still found it hard to believe that he had taken an idea, a wild dream that could quickly have become a nightmare and made it into reality. That was one of the reasons she loved him, the main reason. Not entirely true she had thought, he has other qualities.

She had jumped as he put his cup and saucer on the coffee table with some force, got up from the leather armchair and sat beside her on the settee.

'Look Tracey, I think we need to talk about where we're up to. Get some things clear.'

She had leaned back in the cushions and studied his clear grey eyes. What was coming? She could read no hint. She could reach out and touch him, stroke his face. If he recoiled, what then? Come on man, spit it out.

'Look. Things have moved incredibly fast over the past few months. I've moved on, from a lonely man who retired with so many doubts to this rapidly moving life which I could never have dreamed of.'

'I know. I've been with you.'

'Yes, you have. But this is only the beginning.'

The atmosphere was tense. What was he trying to say? Goodbye? She waited. After a long silence she had spoken.

'Doug, it's more than a beginning. Much more. Look what you have achieved.'

True, he had achieved a hell of a lot. In twelve short months he had moved from a lonely retired widower to helping so many needy people in the depressed town of Maidenbury. Starting with a mobile soup kitchen, he had then rented a shop and turned it into a centre for the lonely and hungry. With an ever growing group of people. Helped by Thelma and Wally, advised by Pastor Jim who had walked the walk before him in a town near where his Pilot was stored. Not forgetting Tracey's support.

It all came back to Tracey. He had feelings for her but were they as deep as hers? This was the problem, he wasn't sure. He wondered what to do, what to say. He was not a man to shy away from decisions but this was different. He had mourned Mary who passed away from an inoperable brain tumour, faced retirement shortly afterwards, moved into the little cottage, started again. Built something he felt called to do, 'The Happening'. Struggled and then it had all come together. Perhaps he should take time to evaluate his emotions, they were all over the place at the moment. He needed to be sure. That was only fair to both of them. He could feel her eyes scanning his face. He glanced down at Ruby who munched the biscuits Tracey had provided, the latter not bothering about the carpet. Ruby was a clean eater… oh stop it man, focus!

He had looked at Tracey. 'Well, I don't know Tracey. So much has happened. Maybe I need, we need, to take stock. Not rush into anything.'

Rush! Oh please say you love me, Dougie! I know I love you. I want to hold you, kiss you, make it all go away. She sensed this wasn't the time for big decisions, knew he could not be pushed. Better to back off and wait. Again.

She had taken a deep breath.

'OK Dougie, I understand. Really I do. Take time to run everything through in your mind, my darling. It will all work out. It will, believe me it will.'

'I'm sorry, I really am Tracey. Thank you for being so understanding.'

She had smiled. Always understanding, that's me. She dived in, changing the subject.

'Oh, there's something I was going to talk to you about. You know who are new MP is, Peter Barker. Well I'm interviewing him next week, going to write in the Chronicle about his past and what he hopes to achieve in the future. Why don't you come and meet him, I'm sure he'd like to hear about what you're doing in his constituency. Tuesday at 4pm. Shall I pick you up at 3.30? If you want to go, that is.'

Doug thought about her invitation. Why not? He kissed her on the cheek with a sigh and left, Ruby happily tagging along at his side. Walkies, good one Dad.

∝

The afternoon was starting to brighten as he and Ruby were driven to the MP's constituency office in Maidenbury. Ruby quite enjoyed her place in the Midget behind the front seats, especially when the top was down. Doug peered at the neglected buildings and deserted shops as Tracey steered them to the office. He thought about the large rented shop he had turned into the community centre and realised that the MP's office was only a few doors down. Another ex-shop.

They walked into the office and were met by a lady in her mid-fifties. Doug was more than impressed at first glance. Her attractive kind face was framed by a two-tone layered hairstyle that made her look younger, with matching discrete make-up. She obviously took care of her appearance without appearing too fussy and self-opinionated. Her twinkling blue eyes studied him through modern, light-coloured spectacle frames. She wore a neatly tailored light grey business suit; jacket and skirt.

Doug felt he needed to say something. 'Good afternoon. I have come here with Tracey Harrison from the Chronicle to see Mr Barker. We have an appointment. Oh I hope it's alright, I've brought my dog Ruby with me.'

She smiled at him as she held out her hand. 'Oh yes, Mr Barker is expecting you. Ruby will be fine, no problem. We get quite a few dogs in here. My name is Sally Metcalf, Mr Barker's assistant. Welcome.'

Her hand was soft and warm. He didn't want to let go but saw Tracey holding hers out. Ruby wagged her tail. Sally crossed to a door and knocked gently. They heard a 'Come in' and were ushered into the MP's surgery with introductions.

Peter Barker got up from behind his desk with outstretched hand. He indicated two chairs in front of the desk and sat down. He was slim, early thirties with keen, expressive hazel eyes and dark well-trimmed hair.

'Good to meet you Tracey, I like your editorials. And you Mr Spencer. You are quite famous in these parts.'

'I don't know about that. I do my best to help.'

'You certainly do. Strange our paths haven't crossed before now. After all, we're only a few doors away.'

Tracey broke in. 'That's why I want you to meet Doug, to hear about his work here.'

A short silence ensued. Doug was starting to get embarrassed, Peter clearly wanted to hear more.

'Is it alright if I take some notes, Mr Barker?' Tracey asked.

This could turn out better than expected, she thought. Not

just an interview with the new MP but a story about his meeting with a significant constituent.

'Please do. And I'm Peter by the way, no formality here. Well Doug, I'm all ears. Really looking forward to hearing about your work.'

There was a tap on the door and Sally entered with a bowl of water which she placed before Ruby.

'Can I get you some tea, or coffee?'

Peter looked enquiringly at the others who agreed on coffee. 'Coffee for me too, please Sally.'

She departed, returning with a tray laden with cups, saucers, teaspoons, milk, sugar and a matching plate of biscuits. With a matching coffee pot. Doug watched her pour three cups and his eyes followed her as she left the room. Calm efficiency.

Tracey interrupted his thoughts. 'OK Doug, the floor is yours,' as she lifted her cup.

Where to begin, Doug wondered. The beginning seems a good place. OK, here goes. As he spoke, Peter looked steadily at him over the rim of his cup, then put it in the saucer on the desk as his eyebrows raised higher and higher. He was obviously interested and impressed.

Doug told him about getting the idea to start a mobile soup kitchen in the centre of the town, how it grew with helpers into renting one of the many disused shops and turning it into a more permanent centre with wholesome meals and somewhere to meet. With a singalong after meals, hymns old and modern led by a small choir. And a tiny chapel if anyone wanted to talk. He said he had been surprised how many liked to sit in silence in the chapel and how many come to the centre every day for help and advice.

When he had finished, the MP stared at him in silence for a moment. 'Well Doug, you're certainly meeting a big need in this town. Well done and thank you for having the vision to get it started. I suppose it's not simply the down and outs who come to you but families as well. There's so much need here.'

'Yes there is. And I feel there is more to do. If I have more ideas, can I count on your support?'

'Of course, any time.'

'Thank you. Well, I'll let Tracey get down to what she came here to do. Thanks for your time. I'll wait for you outside, Tracey.'

They shook hands and he left with Ruby. He hesitated as they walked to the main door, smiling at Sally as she sat typing in her little reception office. She turned to him.

'I hope you're not leaving without telling me about what you've been doing!'

'No, well, eh…'

'Sit down! Time for another brew. Tea or coffee?'

He was just about to leave half an hour later when Tracey appeared, putting her notebook into her handbag.

As they walked to her car, Tracey commented, 'That went well, for you and for me.'

'Yes, nice man. I think he'll be really good for this town.' He glanced at his watch. 'Tell you what, I think I'll go straight to the centre. No point in you driving us home, we'll only have a few minutes and then be back here again.' He turned towards the centre with Ruby.

'OK. How'll you get home later?'

'Someone will give me a lift. Oh, I'm on Gerald's way home. No problem.'

She knew Gerald, the choirmaster at the village church who had discovered Thelma's voice. His wife Alice was Doug's first supporter and encouraged so many to help him. She briefly watched their retreat and turned towards her car.

Chapter Two

Breakfast time. Ruby sat impatiently by her bowl in the kitchen. Here he comes, I can hear his footsteps on the landing. He wasn't easy to get up today, had to drag the duvet off twice. Her tail wagged in excitement as Dad entered, smoothing his hair as he headed for the coffee percolator.

Automatically he opened a cupboard, pulled out a tin of dog food, with a big yawn. Ruby turned her head to one side. Service without a smile this morning, charming. Her bowl filled, she dug in. Doug rinsed his mug in the sink, poured a coffee and stared into space as he leaned against the work surface.

Ruby wondered why he was humming. Why did he keep saying 'Mmm, could be' every few bars? This was like his boring time in the clickie room. Soon after they first met and Dad brought her home from that dumpie place, he would spend ages in that clickie room, clicking in front of that light thingie.

Wriggling in his old office chair, moving in circles, hitting the wall and rebounding.

That was when Doug was trying to write a book about his past, fulfilling his promise to Mary. Staring at the screen, typing on the keyboard, pressing the delete button. He had said to Mary that when he retired he would write a book about his past ministry. She had imagined an autobiography of success stories. He wasn't sure and the more he wrote the more he felt in the main it had all been a waste of time, pointless. He had played the game and the result was not a win, not even a draw, just defeat at every turn. In the end he had pressed the delete button to remove every trace. He had given a wry smile, or was it a grimace, when he did it. Deleted the past, looking to the future.

He moved into his small study and sat behind the desk, his office chair protesting under the strain. Ruby followed and lay beside his chair in anticipation. Probably click click click again. She never could understand the endless clicks and the intense way Dad stared at that bright light in front of him. Something seems a bit off, but what?

Doug pushed the keyboard away to make space for an A4 notepad, looking for a biro. There it was, under the screen. He started writing, filled one page then flipped the page over to start another. He glanced at the photos of his daughters Angela and Beth with his three grandchildren. And the main photo of Mary in the middle. The girls had visited him in the summer with Mark, Jane and Sarah who had played happily with Ruby in the garden. He hoped he would see them again soon.

He continued to write on the pad, making a long list. He was conscious of the number of families with children who were coming for a meal at the centre. It had all started as a refuge for homeless people who need a square meal, warmth and social contact. Things were moving in another direction, not to change what had been set up but branching out. He had a vision of using the centre during the day to provide food to needy families, free or very cheap. He looked at his to do list. Who to contact and get on board, possible sources of food, opening hours, helpers. What had he forgotten? Tracey would help with publicity. He needed to talk with Sally too, she seemed the sort of person he could bounce ideas off. Peter Barker was an obvious choice to get it all moving, he would definitely burn for a food bank.

Tracey and Sally. That could be a sticking point. Need to do some thinking on that one. He looked at Ruby, her tail happily banging the carpet. Stay a doggie Ruby; being a human is so difficult, so many decisions, so divisive. He returned to the pad as thought after thought flowed into his mind.

The evening was as busy as ever. Doug lost count at one hundred and forty-eight. Wally strolled over as he was helping to clear the front of the room for the music. Thelma stopped chatting as she saw them and went over.

'Great grub Doug, the sausage and mash was ace!' Wally grinned. 'And that roly poly, wow!'

'Yeah, the catering team get better and better,' Thelma added.

Doug loved this couple. He would always associate them with the Pilot, finding them in that derelict caravan by a river while he was out walking Ruby. They had been to check on the classic in the lock- up. That reminded him, he must get her up here. But where could he keep her? He had no garage.

In his mind he returned to their first meeting. Thelma's matted fair hair had hung over her face, Wally's long dark hair disheveled and straggly. Uncertain whether he was growing a beard or not, probably just unkept bum fluff.

They had met at the children's home where they had been placed. Both had been in care as their new stepmothers did not want them in the family. They had run away together and kept under the council radar until they reached the age of sixteen.

Instinctively, Doug liked them straight away. Rough around the edges but hearts of gold. They were intelligent but clearly their lack of education had left a mark. They certainly had no difficulty in expressing themselves, often in colourful language.

As they had made a fuss of Ruby, Wally explained they were on probation for shoplifting. They liked their probation officer who they saw as a father figure. Top guy, let them use the shower at the probation offices before sessions and visited the caravan once a month with food and secondhand clothes. He was trying to find them a flat but that looked pretty hopeless. As was the possibility of employment. Now they had a flat in Maidenbury and jobs. Thanks to their new probation officer, Bob Planter.

They were off probation now and doing very well. Thelma worked in the local supermarket as a cashier, Wally at a car wash. They had been invaluable in setting up the centre; Wally counselling people, using his past experience to mentor those in a similar situation. And Thelma, well Doug would never forget Gerald's joy when he heard her sing for the first time. He had almost shouted in delight, 'My dear, you have a unique talent. Amazing, truly amazing! Your mezzo soprano range is incredible.' Now she led the small choir every evening, after the food had been served and remains cleared away.

Helpers, including many of the diners, were clearing away at that moment in preparation for the singing. *Nearer, My God, to Thee* was sung with gusto every evening. It always touched Doug that a hymn associated with the sinking of the Titanic, some survivors reporting that the ship's string ensemble played the hymn as the vessel sank, could move these sinking folk.

Here we go. Thelma was ready…

Chapter Three

Doug sat at the kitchen table, watching the washing machine go round and round. The load would be clean when he took it out, until the next time. Dusting, vacuuming, washing were necessities and a sort of comfort, needed doing because there is no choice. Yes, there are choices but denying the necessities of life doesn't keep things moving. They just pile up until the obvious becomes reality. I need a clean shirt, socks...

He took a sip from his coffee mug. Am I a mug? Or have I been a mug for most of my life and now things have developed as they were meant to, progressed to the point of no return. Tracey would say don't put yourself down all the time. Mary would have said how proud she was. Sally, well he didn't know Sally all that well. But they would work well together, he felt that instinctively. Go with your instinct.

He thought of words he read recently. *For the planet and*

for all living beings to move forward, we can rely on nothing less than an inherent original goodness and a universally shared dignity. Original goodness, a universally shared dignity. Where did that fit in with his attenders at the centre, with the families overflowing the grey high rise flats, the endless need. It doesn't have to be like that, it just is. A world full of need. Everyone gets born, makes the best of often a bad lot, gets on with life. Because what choice is there. Some make it, some don't. Some are happy, some not. People so often ask is God dead, is he asleep, does he care? How can the hungry, the grieving, those dying of an incurable illness, those with little or nothing, believe in an inherent original goodness or shared universal dignity?

Even the animal world has its haves and have nots. Ruby had been through grief and sadness, experienced loneliness and rejection. But things had turned around, she had found him and he rejoiced in her company. That came from a one-off visit to a dog shelter, a response on both sides and a willingness to try to find a better life. Together.

There was much more to her love than being fed and watered, given shelter. There was trust, hope, just being, abiding. So much to learn from animals he thought, they have a soul. Treated like an animal. Stupid words, some animals are treated with the love and respect they deserve. Some humans are treated worse than animals. Humans and animals have a universally shared dignity. Depending on what they are given to start with and how they respond to the hand they are dealt. Acceptance or challenge, a desire to make things better. To overcome. Talent is a raw gift from inherent original goodness, it can be nurtured or ignored in family life yet it will always materialise into its full potential. Though there will always be a greater talent, there is always someone better, more talented, somewhere. Fact of life.

Because there are more effective soup kitchens and centres elsewhere, better organised food banks, is that an excuse not to try? *The best criticism of the bad is the practice of the better.* More words he had read recently. Easy to criticise, to pull down, to make excuses. It takes guts to recognise the bad and make an effort to do something better. Was that what he was doing, recognising the bad in his past experiences and try to make something better? How is 'better' graded? By results. The proof of the pudding, one man's meat is another man's poison. Justice, in its broadest sense, is the principle that people receive what they deserve. Was he fighting for justice? Different meaning for different people.

As the washing machine came to the end of its cycle, Doug groaned. He wasn't sure whether it was the thought of removing the clothes and putting them away, or because his mind wouldn't stop spinning.

'Come on girl, let's go walkies.' He stood up and headed for the front door. She got there before him.

They walked to the village and beyond. It was a cloudy November day with a light breeze. As Ruby trotted at his side, she stopped to sniff the grass verges then caught him up, a familiar routine. Doug thought of the early days when they were out for walks, how he kept her on a lead. Now she ran free in trust. Trust. It had to be earned. Who did he trust, who could he trust? Who did he want to trust? He had trusted Tracey but she had let him down.

He had trusted Mary implicitly, she was the only person he had ever fully trusted. His work had been filled with rumours, exaggerations, lies even. But at the end of the day he could sit down with Mary and analysis it all, find some truth, talk openly about what was going on and find some peace. Hear comforting words of wisdom. In that sense she was irreplaceable. Decades in a relationship can be replaced by a new relationship. Well some can, but deep understanding, knowing each other's thoughts, takes time. Sometimes never.

They were almost at Tracey's house. He wasn't sure whether he had intended this destination or it just happened. Come on Doug, things don't just happen, they happen for a reason. He paused, staring at the cul-de-sac with her house on the left. Ruby knew where they were, her tail had stopped wagging.

Maybe she was out. It was lunchtime and that was unlikely. He thought about turning round, not sure what he was going to say. She would listen to his plans for a food bank, be supportive, have ideas. As to talking about their relationship... what was there to say? They were good friends, had similar interests. The white MG Midget was parked in the driveway. Point of no return.

He rang the doorbell. Tracey opened the door and looked at him in surprise. After a few seconds, she spoke.

'Well this is a surprise. Come in.'

They stood in the hallway, Doug not knowing what to say.

Closing the door she said, 'Well we can't stand here all day' and went into the lounge, sitting on the settee. Doug followed, sitting in an armchair with Ruby by his side. Tracey looked at him with an enquiring expression.

'Oh, we were out walking, and eh, we ended up here.' Sounds a bit lame he thought. 'Well actually, I want to talk to you.' Lamer and lamer.

She did not speak.

This is awkward. Get on man, for goodness sake say something.

'Well I want to run something past you, if that's alright.' Silence.

He patted Ruby for comfort, reassurance and launched in. He told her about his hope to start a food bank and who he would need to contact, the list he had made and anyone he might have missed.

Still she did not speak, staring at him as she processed the information. Nothing about their relationship, just practicalities. As friends. What did she expect? To be gathered into his arms, kissed, made love to even? She had enjoyed going fishing with her father and knew you have to cast bait to get a reaction. Perhaps this was the time to get a catch, or lose it. Nothing ventured...

'OK, well my first reaction is that you have more than enough to do. How on earth are you going to organise a food bank with everything else on your plate. Oh I don't deny there's a need, a big need, but come on Doug, get real.'

Ouch. That wasn't what he wanted to hear. She had a point though.

She cast her line. 'Actually I have a friend, someone I met doing an interview for work. Nice chap, just divorced. We've been for a couple of meals and get on well.' She purposely did not use the 'date' word.

Doug didn't know what to reply. Was this his way out? But he didn't want to lose her friendship. Not because she had useful contacts but, well, they had come a long way together. The centre would have been much harder to establish without her support, more than that she had helped him to pull himself together.

He had been a mess. She had been and still is a good friend. All that is true, but it doesn't always make for a close relationship. A romantic one. Well, it might but that's not always how it works out. For him anyway.

He knew he had to say something. 'Oh, I'm happy for you Tracey. I hope it works out, really I do.'

The one that got away. He could have said nothing, come over and swept her into his arms. Been jealous. There was no hint of jealousy in his voice. You can't make people love you, they do or they don't. It happens. For Doug, the 'Happening' was the centre of his world. Best thing that happened to him. Something had happened for her though, there is no denying that. Genuinely happened. She was in love. With this guy who could be so close yet so distant, so together yet so apart. So intelligent yet so vulnerable. Oh my Dougie, we would make such a good couple. But if you can't see it, won't see it, then…

'Yes, well, it's early days. Anything can happen. It's good to have friends.'

'Absolutely.' He paused. 'So you don't think a food bank is a good idea?'

She almost laughed. 'I didn't say that. It just needs some thinking about. If it is going to work.'

He looked relieved, like a small boy needing reassurance that his dream will come true. She melted.

'Of course it will work Dougie, I know you will make it work.'

That was what he needed to hear.

'OK, thanks for that.' Pause. 'I'll get on then.'

She nodded. 'You do that. And let me know how it goes.'

'Sure will. I can count on your help and advice then?'

'Of course you can.'

He got up, kissed her on the cheek. She stared at them as they left the room, heard the front door close behind them. A tear rolled down her cheek, then another. Soon she was weeping uncontrollably.

Mid-morning and Doug was tidying up at the centre, checking the food would be sufficient for the expected hundred plus needy who would come that evening. Lamb stew, with potatoes and carrots all willingly provided by the only remaining supermarket in town. Ruby scampered happily around, approving the supplies and hoping for a few bones later.

The usual morning run of people seeking advice had gone away content and everything looked straight. He was locking up when he paused, glanced towards the constituency office. Why not?

As he entered, Sally looked up with a smile. 'Hello Doug, nice to see you again'.

He wanted to reply 'To see you nice' but resisted. Instead he smiled back and mumbled, 'Hello Sally. Just been getting ready for this evening and thought I'd pop in to see you.'

'I'm glad you did. Anything special on your mind?' She paused with the files she had been sorting into the filing cabinet, looked at him expectantly.

'Well, eh. Not really. Well actually yes, but I'm sure you're busy.'

'Nothing that can't wait. Peter is away this week so I'm on

my own. Fancy a coffee, I'm sure you need a drink after the queue of people I saw going into the centre.'

'Sure, that would be nice.' So she had been keeping an eye on him. He found that comforting.

He sat down as she put the kettle on. Normally he would have felt awkward but didn't.

'Or would you like tea?'

'No no, coffee's fine thanks. If you're having one.'

The pleasantries of domesticity. As she handed him a cup and saucer their hands touched briefly. *I want to hold your hand* came into his head. He felt like a teenager again, carefree with the world at his feet. She glided her office chair from behind her desk so she could sit next to him.

'I'm very glad you popped in Doug, I've just had some bad news.' She sipped her coffee slowly.

Doug put his cup and saucer on the desk, a concerned expression on his face.

'I'm sorry to hear that, Sally. Do you want to talk about it?'

Her ex father-in-law had just been killed in a car accident. Sally was a widow and had kept in touch with Greg who was a widower. Her husband John had been killed six years previously in a car accident, so the news had opened up old wounds. The similarities were astounding. Greg was seventy-eight years old and had formed a relationship with a married mother of three, although she claimed that she would not leave her family. They went line-dancing together. When she didn't turn up one week, he went looking for her. He was an advanced driver and never touched alcohol when driving. Whilst out looking for her, he apparently drove the wrong way down a dual carriageway and hit another car. Both drivers died instantly.

Doug took her hand.

'There's more though,' she said, almost in a whisper.

She took a deep breath.

'My husband John was hit by another car and died instantly. The other driver was drunk. I found out later that John was on his way to meet his girlfriend, also married. Apparently they had been seeing each other for almost a year.' She paused, unable to look at him.

Doug squeezed her hand and touched her cheek, gently pulling her face towards his. He gazed into her eyes and said softly 'Sally, I am so sorry. This must be bringing back so many sad memories.'

She tried to smile but the pain held her back. She let him move her head to his shoulder, whimpered slightly when he kissed her cheek. They rubbed cheeks for a moment, then embraced in a long kiss.

'I think we'd better move away from that big window' she gasped, not wanting to stop.

He kissed her lips briefly. 'Let's go to my place. It's quiet there.'

'OK. Let me lock up first.'

He drove in embarrassed silence. Their heads were in a whirl, each trying to process what had been said and the reaction. Ruby snuggled on the rear seat, happy that Dad was happy. She sensed a glow coming from him that she had not felt before.

He pulled into the small driveway in front of the cottage and stopped the engine. What now? They both looked through the windscreen, not knowing what to say. He took her hand and pulled her towards him, kissing her lips. Their kiss was long and passionate. Doug sensed that they both wanted, needed more.

He opened her door and escorted her into the cottage. As he looked into her eyes he felt her warm acquiescence and lead her upstairs. Beside his bed they hugged and caressed, their kisses growing in a crescendo of passion. They fell onto the bed and all their pain melted in a joyful desire that neither could control, or wanted to.

Later, Doug lay back on the pillow, Sally resting on his shoulder as she fondled his chest. If this was a dream he didn't want to wake up. No, it was real. Mary would be so happy for him. Tracey? Well they had been, still were, just friends. He felt a nip of guilt but there was no need. He hadn't led her on, no promises made. They enjoyed each other's company, if she hoped for more... stop right there! Don't spoil the moment with a guilt trip.

He bent over and kissed Sally's cheek, then her lips. They were content just to lie together, outside time. Their past did not matter, only the present. And the future? Let that take care of itself, they had found each other.

Ruby was asleep in front of the log fire in the lounge, her tail happily thumped the carpet as she dreamed. Strange noises coming from upstairs, not sure what, but no worries. Dad's safe, and happy.

Chapter Four

It was late. The helpers had gone home; cooks, cleaners and what he laughingly called 'the minders' who made sure the assembly were drink and drug free. The choir had left too. Thelma and Wally were in the main room putting the final touches to tidying up, as Ruby ate the scraps which was her contribution to the process.

Doug sat on the back row of the small chapel, staring at the Cross on the tiny table at the front. The words of a song came into his thoughts:

> *If I could fall into the sky*
> *Do you think time would pass me by?*
> *'Cause you know I'd walk a thousand miles*
> *If I could just see you*
> *If I could just hold you tonight*

These words had crossed his mind so often after Mary had passed away. *If I could just see you. If I could just hold you tonight.* Twenty-six years of holding her, knowing her, being with her. Sharing so much. He sighed. He had fallen into the sky, fallen a long way, suffocated almost. Almost. It seemed like he had walked a thousand miles over the past twelve months.

Why couldn't he feel content, rest on his laurels? Be at peace. The nagging feeling was a new experience, something he had rarely felt during his ministry. That was over; retired from playing the game, being the man everybody expected but nobody appreciated. A clown in the big top.

Was he praying? Perhaps. Prayer can be so shallow; self-centred, so misunderstood. All about me instead of Him. Give me peace, for God's sake give me peace! Is that too much to ask? What more do you want?

There was something else though, something he instinctively felt was about to happen. So much had been achieved, yet that was not the end of the story. Would it ever end? There is always layer upon layer, nothing is ever complete. What though? What was this nagging feeling?

Sally stood in the doorway, looking at him with an expression of sympathy, understanding. He thought she had gone home with the others. Why had she returned? She sat next to him and gently took his hand in silence, holding it in her lap. A feeling of amazing peace overwhelmed him, a feeling he had not known for a long time.

∝

As he looked at his list for the food bank, thinking about Sally, the words *It's a great day, watch some b*****d ruin it* came into his head. Comes from glass half empty people, though he wasn't certain that he always considered his half full. Some days it was full, others pretty empty. But that was his decision.

He sat in the clickie room, rocking in his office chair which wasn't made for rocking but did from old age. Ruby lay at his feet dozing, waiting for the bright light and accompanying clicks. Silence. Just creaking from the chair, the odd spin as he swung to the music on the radio.

'Our bowl's about full today kidda.'

Bowl? Food? Suddenly she was fully awake in expectation. She got a treat in consolation. Breakfast had just been served and it was quite a while until teatime. Oh well, back to sleep then.

The 'phone rang. As he turned down the radio, Doug had a feeling bad news was on the way. He wasn't wrong.

'Doug, Doug, it's Thelma. Wally's been arrested!'

He wasn't expecting that one. Both Wally and Thelma had been charged in the past with shoplifting and placed on probation. They had served their time, had their supervision orders transferred from Longmire to Maidenbury probation service when they moved to help him with the centre, cooperated fully and received a lot of support and help in the process. Shining examples who had turned their lives around.

A sneaking worry broke into his head as questions spun - what was he accused of and could he have done it? He was sure of Thelma, she had transformed into a model citizen. Wally? He'd never be a model citizen but he was a good lad. He pushed nagging doubts to the back of his mind.

'Oh no. What's he charged with?'

'Armed robbery, Doug. My Wally wouldn't do that, you

know that Doug. Oh shit, this isn't happening. What we gonna do?'

'Where is he now?'

'The local nick. We gotta do somethin.' She was very close to tears.

He asked her to calm down, this must be a mistake. He would go to the police station right away. She seemed calmer, knowing he would help. She never doubted that for a moment, but her experience of authority frightened her. They had toughed it out together, ducked and dived, but never separately. Not since they met at the children's home. They had run away together, kept under the radar until being caught for shoplifting. Two packets of biscuits and a loaf of bread.

She was at the flat, had to ring work sick. He told her he would call round as soon as he had some news. She sounded more together when she rang off.

He reached for the telephone index and thumbed the cards. He found the number he was looking for and dialed. Please be in Bob. It answered after three rings. Bob Planter had been a good help to Doug when he started the mobile soup kitchen and later in setting up the centre.

It was Bob's mobile. He spoke in a quiet voice, explaining that he was in the magistrates' court waiting area. He listened without interruption as Doug told him about Thelma's call.

'Armed robbery? I can't see that. I'll have a word here, the sergeant should know something. I should be out of here in about forty minutes. I'll bell you when I'm on my way to the police station.' The line went dead.

What a mess. There was no way he could think Wally would be involved in anything so reckless. Daft sometimes, yes. But heavy criminal stuff, no way. It wasn't in his nature.

Ruby was waiting at the front door, she knew something wasn't right from Dad's tone of voice. She followed him to the car, jumping into the passenger seat when he opened the door. OK, ride now, walkies later. Doug backed out and headed for Maidenbury, deep in thought.

He parked near the police station and waited for the call. It was only five minutes in coming.

'I'm just parking up, meet you at the front in five.'

Doug left Ruby in the car, with the front windows partly open. It wasn't hot weather and she was asleep. Her tail twitched as Doug gently closed his door but she didn't stir.

He saw Bob approaching and went to meet him. They shook hands.

'Bloody hell, I don't believe this Doug. The sergeant at court said he's charged with armed robbery of a petrol station, with two other guys. We'd better go in and see what's happening.'

They went to the desk and were taken down to the cells. Bob was well known and often visited the cells. As the door swung open, Wally jumped up from the bunk and looked at them anxiously. The door banged shut, the officer stating 'Ten minutes' as he departed.

'We haven't got long Wally, so let's get started. How did you get involved in this, and who are you charged with?'

Wally sat back down as he looked at Bob. He looked terrified.

'I ain't involved with nuffin Bob, honest. I never did nuffin.'

'OK, so tell us the names of the other two.'

'Johnnie Dawson and Danny O'Reilly.'

Bob nodded. Those two he could believe, they had gone through the system and come out the other side. Had custodial sentences as long as his arm. Wally didn't fit their profiles, they were hard guys. He looked at his watch. Doug sat next to Wally, Bob standing expectantly in front of them with his arms crossed.

'Those guys are bad news guys. How did you get involved with them?'

Wally shivered, wringing his hands. 'I never, I only know of em. Never seen em, never even met em, like. Never.'

It had started at the centre. He had been helping one of the homeless men to get into a shelter near Maidenbury, a council place which was always full. He had offered to talk to the warden and put in a good word, grab the next available bed. Then he had heard two men talking about something big going down that night at the petrol station where he worked. Just before it closed. He had looked at his watch and realised it would be in the next half an hour. He'd run straight there and two guys were about to rob it with guns. They were looking round to make sure the coast was clear, pulled scarves over their faces and moved in.

He should have waited but he knew the girl attendant would be scared stiff. He didn't think, just ran to the doors and stood in front of the guys. The automatic doors opened and one of the men pushed him in. He had a scarf over his mouth and nose because he'd had a chest infection and it was a cold night. The girl didn't recognise him at first.

A guy had been coming out of the Gents at the side of the building, saw what was going down and rung the police.

The robbers ran to the doors when two police cars arrived but they were pushing him around and it looked like they were in it together. As the doors opened, the three of them were together and the cops nicked them. Turned out the guns were dummies. He turned imploringly to Doug.

'You believe me don't you Doug, you gotta believe me!'

The cell door opened and the officer stood in the doorway. Bob nodded and walked out. Doug told Wally not to worry, they would sort it out, as he followed. The door banged shut.

Doug began to speak as they went down the short corridor to the stairs but Bob put a finger to his lips, mouthing, 'Wait!'

Outside, Bob breathed a long sigh.

'Crock in't. Load of bollocks.'

Doug wasn't certain whether he meant what Wally had told them, or if he was considered innocent.

'Dawson and O'Reilly are going to drag him in, probably try to blame him. It don't look good.'

Doug was nonplussed, way out of his depth. This was the real world; dark and relentless, unforgiving, brutal. He had to see Thelma, though what he was going to say escaped him. He had some thinking to do on his way there. Bob said he needed to run the whole affair past a colleague, come up with a plan of campaign. Talk to a solicitor too.

'You do believe him don't you, Bob?'

'Sounds plausible but the prosecution won't be impressed.' He saw Doug's downcast expression. 'Yes, I do. But that isn't going to change the situation, the facts right now are pretty damning.'

Doug said he was going to see Thelma and asked if he wanted to come, but he had to get the ball rolling on the defence. He would see her later.

Ruby stirred as he opened his door, yawned and licked his cheek. He put his hands on the wheel and slumped his head onto them. After a few minutes he started the engine, paused and turned it off.

'I think we might be better leaving the car here and walking, safer.'

Walkies!

$$\propto$$

Two blocks of high-rise flats dominated the town landscape. Dilapidated, ignored, abandon hope all ye who enter here type of buildings. Thelma lived on the top floor of the block with the most paint peeling off. With a bit of luck the lift might be working. It was. As they ascended, Doug thought about who he could get involved to help. As the lift doors creaked slowly open, he pulled out his 'phone.

Call to Tracey, she would get an article in the Chronicle. Then call to Sally. Tell Peter, get the MP on the case. OK, who else? He couldn't think of anyone at that moment, most bases covered. Bob would be working hard making a case for the defence. A case for what? Circumstantial evidence. Wrong place, wrong time. His thoughts turned to Thelma as they approached the flat. What a stink, stale urine and worse in the lift. Ruby's nose had been twitching violently as he tried to hold his breath.

Here we are. He took a deep breath and knocked on the door.

Thelma threw it open and hugged him in the doorway. He could feel her body trembling. They followed her into the cramped lounge. Doug sat on the worn sofa as Ruby wondered round sniffing everywhere. Not a palace but an improvement on the caravan which had long ago gone to the tip. At least

Thelma tried to keep it clean and looked after what old furniture they had.

'How's it looking Doug, when can he come home?'

He focused on a patch of threadbare carpet in the centre of the floor. After a moment he looked at her with what he hoped was an encouraging smile.

'We've got a lot of people working to sort this out, Thelma. People who know what they're doing.'

He told her about his visit to the police station with Bob Planter and how Wally had explained his side of events. He couldn't hide the fact that Wally was at the scene and got involved, albeit by chance. The two men who had perpetrated the crime were well known to the police and wouldn't tell the truth about Wally. So there was a long way to go but there was hope. He wouldn't be home for a while, though.

No point in dressing up the facts, that wouldn't help. She was quite bright and would rather know what they were up against than be told lies and given false hope. She nodded slowly, taking it all in.

'I understand Doug, or rather I don't but I know you and others are doing what you can. Guess I'll just have to be patient, hope for the best.' There were tears in her eyes. She had had bad experiences with authority, they both had. Luck never seemed to be on their side, always against them.

She looked like a little lost soul in the fading armchair that had seen better days.

'Look Thelma, moping around here isn't going to help. Why don't you go back to work, it will take your mind off things.'

She nodded. The manager had told her she could have time off but she wanted to go back. She'd be at the centre tonight and would go back to work tomorrow morning.

'Good, see you later Thelma. If you need me, or want to talk, you know where I am.'

When they left, the lift had stopped working. Easier to walk down the stairs than struggle up.

Chapter Five

Doug stood at the back and looked round the centre. Meals served, all cleared away, music and singing done. Thelma had performed to her usual high standard. He watched her as she waved and smiled with the choir and musicians, guitars and drums, the clapping and shouts a pure tribute to their magnificence. A world within a world, a society all its own.

Lost, found, resurrected. That's the word, resurrected. Something that is inactive, disused, or forgotten. To bring something back to life. It doesn't have to be perfect, perfection is in the eye of the beholder. Do money, power, social standing, fame make perfection? Those are the bench marks. Aren't they?

He gazed at Thelma. A young woman born into nothing, neglected and rejected. Found companionship with a young man of similar dubious beginnings. Struggled to keep their head above water in swirling rivers of ups and downs. Dashed by rocks, blocked by boulders, forced under but always coming up with new intake of breath. Sometimes gasping but ever hoping. This time there was a heavy boulder weighing them both down.

He had to see Sally, talk things over, touch normality. When he had checked and locked up, he would call round. Their relationship had gone beyond formality; dates, small talk, trying to impress, showing the best side. Now it was me as I am, warts and all. A good place to be; comfortable, relaxing, safe, secure.

They headed for the neat bungalow which was just before the village, on the Maidenbury side. Ruby knew the way. She sat on the passenger seat, her seat, looking through the windscreen. Well Dad, good choice. Treats. Yum yum. Are we there yet?

Sally was in. She opened the front door in her lilac dressing-gown and slippers.

'That's a sight for sore eyes,' he murmured as he hugged her.

'I had a feeling you'd call round.' She took his hand and led him into the lounge, pulling him onto the settee. He kissed her lips, stroked her hair and caressed her face at the same time. It seemed like desperation, release, longing, all rolled into one. They lay together in silence, Ruby snuggled down too in front of the hearth.

Sally felt the tension slowly drain from his body. His head lay on her breast, his breathing became more controlled. She wanted to take all his pain away but knew it was the pain that drove him. Fighting injustice, hoping for a better tomorrow, not for himself but for others. There was a nobility she admired yet instinctively feared. For him. There was only one way, to share and support. To try to see the big picture and be there. Be a hand to hold when the going gets tough, the calm in the eye of the storm.

At last she spoke softly, gently squeezing him. 'I guess you're staying tonight.' A rhetorical question, a warm invitation.

Time to get away. See the Pilot and Pastor Jim. Tell him about Wally. A character witness would be good, no doubt Jim would be willing. He had known the couple from the beginning and they had introduced him to Jim.

He had told Sally about Pastor Jim and the Pilot and she was excited to meet them both. It was a Saturday morning and Doug drove to Sally's bungalow early in the morning to collect her as arranged. It was a clear, crisp day, perfect for driving. They would be back in good time for the evening meal at the centre which Thelma was supervising. It would keep her mind occupied, going to work and then straight to the centre.

Sally was at the door when they arrived and Ruby jumped into the back seat. They were off. Doug headed east for the M4 where the traffic was swiftly moving, they would be there in about an hour.

'Well, this is exciting! I really am looking forward to seeing the car and having a drive. And to meeting Jim, of course.'

He had told her all about Jim and his support. And the Pilot, how his father had left it to him with the lockup. That's a point. Where to keep it in the village. It needed to be under cover, the driveway at his cottage would be no good.

She broke into his thoughts. 'I've been thinking Doug, about the car. The garage is empty at my place.' She didn't drive, she had a licence but no immediate need of a vehicle.

'Hey, that would be great! Thanks Sally, another problem solved.'

'Just happy to make you happy,' she smiled. 'I know how much the car means to you.'

That's true. It had meant a lot to his father and Doug had fond memories of sitting in the back seat watching the world go by as his father proudly drove, his mother next to him. The smell of leather upholstery, the chrome door handles, the roar of the V8 engine were all magic.

He pulled into the row of lockups and parked to the side of his. Switching off the engine, he went round to open the passenger door.

'Your carriage awaits, madame,' he bowed ceremoniously.

She followed him to the double doors and he unlocked the padlock, Ruby sniffing the ground. Been here before, nice smells. Happy smells.

He threw open the doors and carefully removed the dust cover.

'Voila!'

'Oh Doug, she's a beauty.' Sally did not know much about cars, let alone classics but she was impressed. The dark blue coachwork was shiny and she peered inside at the beige upholstery.

'Wanna go for a spin?'

'Oh yes please.'

Soon they were purring, or rather roaring, down a dual carriageway and into the country. Ruby lay on the back seat, fascinated by Dad moving that thing up and down. The three speed gearbox lever was expertly moved up and down as Doug drove. Soon they were speeding along.

Sally looked contentedly at his expression, seeing a side she hadn't noticed before. Total absorption mixed with complete relaxation; listening to the engine with his head tilted slightly on one side, glancing at the dials, a smile on his lips.

'Don't suppose you fancy a try?'

'Oh no thanks, I daren't. She's too beautiful for a novice to handle. Needs an expert.'

He shrugged with a smile. This was perfect. The three of them, well four actually, he counted the Pilot as part of his family. He eased off the throttle as he turned into a country lane. Checking the rear-view mirror he pulled over and parked up. He sat looking at her for a few moments. She looked straight ahead but could feel the warmth of his gaze. He gently kissed her cheek.

'Just look at this beautiful countryside. And us here together. It feels like a dream.' She looked at him. 'Is it a dream?'

'Nope. It's reality. If we want it to be.' He took her hand. 'Do we want it to be?'

Her smile of contentment told him the answer.

He looked at the clock on the dashboard. 'Hey, we need to get going. Sorry to break up the dream but reality calls. Better get her back and go to see Jim.'

He put the car in gear and headed back to the lockup. Soon they were on their way in the estate to the centre of Longmire. He parked on the road near Jim's church. He had kept Jim updated on progress during their weekly telephone conversations, had told him about the idea of a food bank, mentioned Sally. They were expected.

Memories flooded back as they entered. The church was part of the centre and was separate from the large hall where hot meals were provided for the needy. They entered the hall. This is where his life changed. That first time he reluctantly came with Thelma and Wally, not knowing what to expect. He had entered as a lonely recently retired Anglican clergyman and left with a remarkable vision.

He remembered his many questions. The answers he had found as his centre had gradually come together. He smiled as he saw the sign on the wall at the front of the building. *Welcome to your Evangelical Church.* The thoughts that had gone through his mind the first time he reluctantly went to meet Jim. To his surprise, finding him down to earth, no frills, genuine and caring.

Belonging to the evangelical wing of the Church of England himself, he had felt joy and fear mixed in anticipation. High Church, Middle Church and Low Church. High Church often higher than the average Roman Catholic Church; Middle being centre of the road Anglicans; Low being often seen as Happy Clappy. All within one complicated denomination.

The struggle within some Church of England diocese with a bishop who would not ordain women to the priesthood, one suffragan (assistant) bishop who might and one low suffragan bishop who would. An unholy mystery to many both inside and outside the denomination. What he had come to call *Outside the inside*, all knocking at the same door but interpreting the scene differently as they grappled within.

Doug looked round. Still the same; a long serving table, three side by side at the far end where hot food was served to a steady stream of eager souls holding plastic trays and mugs. And there he was, Pastor Jim, preparing for the evening.

Jim saw them and came forward, hand outstretched. Early thirties, a striking Jesus lookalike. Well how the Aryan Jesus is portrayed, not the real one with dark hair and eyes. This one was blond, blue-eyed with a short blond beard, clad in jeans and white T-shirt.

Doug had felt instinctively that Sally was a believer and thought it strange that they hadn't actually sat down and talked about it. Not exactly top of the agenda in relationships, such thoughts are not usually put into words. Sally was happy with his centre and the chapel, so he imagined she would be happy here. She certainly looked happy.

Jim shook hands warmly, hugged Sally and patted Ruby whose tail wagged in recognition. Time seemed to have stood still. They talked on the 'phone and Jim had visited the centre and stayed at Doug's cottage, but it was a while since Doug had been here.

'Well Sally, it's great to meet you at last. Doug has told me all about you.'

'All good I hope!'

'I don't know about that,' Doug replied. 'But she does keep me under control, tries at least.'

'This is where it all started Sally. You can blame me,' Jim laughed.

'Oh, I think a higher power was, is involved, don't you.' She looked at them both.

'Let me show you round' offered Jim, then paused. 'No, that's Doug's privilege.'

Doug took her hand and led her round the centre. 'Only difference to ours is the larger kitchen area at the back. And it has a church for regular meetings.'

'The food bank brings the community together, attempts to meet the diverse needs,' added Jim. 'Working families come from all sorts of backgrounds.'

'I want to hear about that Jim, guess you have to start with the need and work outwards from there. But first I have to tell you about Wally.'

Jim led them into the church where they sat on the seats at the front. At first they sat in silence. Then they talked, prayed. Doug told him about Wally and explained how they were trying to help him and support Thelma. Jim said he would do whatever was needed and would gladly appear in court if necessary as a character witness.

Before they left, Jim told them all about the food bank and how it worked.

The couple drove home in thoughtful silence. Eventually Sally spoke.

'Did you get what you wanted? How the food bank is run was very interesting, there's more to it than you think.

'True. Put you off?'

'No way! Just thinking, running it all though in my mind. Making plans.'

'Ah, plans. Planning is important.' He knew that already, thought of his lists, ticking things off then starting a new one. But he liked to hear Sally's thoughts, felt comforted by her support. They were on the right road, weren't they? Where was it leading? Happiness they say is a way of travelling, not a destination. Well he was happy so that's a good signpost. Isn't it? Keep your mind on the road and think of this evening's meeting.

He dropped Sally off at her bungalow, had a quick peep in the garage to make sure it would accommodate the Pilot. He felt

49

a bit guilty with all the things going on to be concentrating on his classic car, but it was another small part of the puzzle solved. The puzzle - so many pieces to fit together. First Wally, that was going to be tricky.

He rang Bob Planter to find out if there is any news.

Good and bad. Wally had been charged and was to appear at the Magistrates' Court the following morning, when he would be remanded to appear at Salisbury Crown Court. Bob had found a good solicitor who had agreed to take the case and would be asking for bail tomorrow. Unlikely to be granted so a further remand in custody to HMP Erlestoke was on the cards. A category C prison, for men considered not to be trusted in open conditions but who are considered unlikely to make a determined escape attempt.

As he entered the centre, Doug thoughtfully put his 'phone back in his jacket pocket. Thelma was helping to prepare a hot stew with boiled potatoes and green beans. She looked up, saw him, left the group of cooks and dashed towards him.

'What's happening Doug?' she implored, wiping her hands on her apron.

Better be straight, no frills. But maybe leave it at tomorrow and see what happens then. He explained that Bob had got a good solicitor and Wally would appear at the Magistrates' Court tomorrow morning. She nodded, seeming to accept what she was told.

'I'll be there, at the court.'

'You can go Thelma but don't expect to be able to talk to him. It will be a very quick hearing. Why don't you think about it.'

"OK. I'll think about it.' She wandered back to the cooks,

turned as if to say something then continued, deep in thought.

Doug hadn't imparted the rest of Bob's information. Convictions for armed robbery average eight years' imprisonment. The other two would probably plead guilty to receive lesser sentences, as they were caught red-handed. Wally had to plead not guilty but there was the strong possibility of a conviction as things stood at the moment. It all boiled down to if the jury would believe him and the competence of his barrister.

He checked round, everything seemed fine. Get the evening over and then make more plans.

Chapter Six

Wally was brought into the dock in handcuffs with his two co-defendants. He looked round, waved as best he could when he spotted Thelma and Doug sitting in the public gallery. This was his first time in such a court, his appearance with Thelma for shoplifting had been in a youth court. Being put on probation had been a good help to them, he had to admit that. But this place, adult court, it looked so serious.

The clerk read out the charge, armed robbery. He asked each defendant in turn to state their name, address, date of birth. The other two went first. When Wally's turn came, he felt all eyes turn on him. He tried to appear calm.

Then it was time to hear their plea.

'John Robert Dawson, you are charged with armed robbery under section 8(1) of the Theft Act 1968. How do you plead?'

'Guilty.'

'Daniel James O'Reilly, you are charged with armed robbery under section 8(1) of the Theft Act 1968. How do you plead?'

'Guilty.'

'Walter Roberts, you are charged with armed robbery under section 8(1) of the Theft Act 1968. How do you plead?'

Wally stared at his solicitor who was watching him with his arm resting over the wooden bench. What should he reply? They had talked about it but the others were saying something different.

The solicitor stood up to address the bench of two men and the woman chairperson.

'My client pleads not guilty, ma'am.' He sat down again.

The three magistrates conferred briefly. The chairperson looked at the defendants, glancing at the papers in front her.

'John Robert Dawson and Daniel James O'Reilly, you will be remanded on bail for sentence to Salisbury Crown Court. Walter Roberts, you are remanded in custody for trial to Salisbury Crown Court. Next case.'

They were ushered out of the dock. Dawson and O'Reilly grinned at each other. As Wally was taken past them to the cells, they mimicked 'Fall guy' in his face.

Doug put his arm round Thelma who was gently sobbing into his handkerchief.

Doug tried to take his mind off things by concentrating on his food bank lists. He had taken Thelma back to work as she insisted, said she needed to keep busy. They all needed to keep busy. He couldn't stop thinking about Wally, being transported on remand to prison in handcuffs. Innocent until proven guilty.

But surely he couldn't be found guilty because he was innocent. Doug had no doubt about his innocence but that didn't mean the jury would think that way. He shuddered, not wanting to go down that road. Years in a prison cell... come on, it hasn't happened yet. May never happen.

They say things come in threes. If two bad things happen in sequence there is a third happy event waiting round the corner. Apparently. Or combinations thereof.

One evening as they were clearing up, Thelma asked Doug for a word as he tied up black bin bags. The centre was empty apart from the helpers and a lady who seemed out of place as she helped clear away. He hadn't seen her before and intended welcoming her. There had been so many new folk that evening and he had spoken with them all, except her.

'OK, I was just about to introduce myself. Do you know her?'

It seemed that Thelma knew her quite well, they had a mutual friend who had invited her to come to Maidenbury. Thelma had felt sorry for her and had invited her to the centre.

'Her name is Serena. She needs help.'

Thelma explained that she didn't have any money and is often hungry. She is an aging prostitute whose children had one by one been taken into care. She had met a Pakistani man in Manchester and they had a baby girl together. The local authority had taken the baby into care. Serena was a recovering alcoholic and her track record was not impressive. She lived in a flat on the same floor as Thelma and her life was chaotic. But Thelma was convinced she was a good mother, if only she could prove it to the powers that be.

'Well, let me meet her and see where we go from there.'

Thelma led him over to Serena and introduced them. He guessed she was in her mid-fifties but appearances can be deceptive. She was forty-three. Her dark hair was bleached with black roots showing through, her make-up heavy.

'Shall we go into the chapel Serena, we can talk there.'

She followed him. He imagined the information Thelma had provided was the tip of the iceberg. At first she was guarded but soon warmed to him. In her broad Manchester accent her words tumbled out. She focused on the present, her relationship with Ashar and their daughter Basma, which means smile. The baby was in foster care and she was trying to get her back. She had done everything the local authority had asked of her, even completed a parenting course. Done alcohol tests which proved she had been off the booze for fifteen months, since meeting Ashar.

During his time at the centre Doug had learned so much, listened to many different life stories and experiences but this was something new. He asked her to tell him about Ashar. She said he is a gentle man who only wanted to help. This had been a new experience for her, most of the men she had known were cheats and liars who only used her. Getting him across to the authorities was very difficult. Her past and the fact that he is an older Muslim man with different beliefs and customs were all stacked against them.

She paused, looking for some response. Thelma had told her that he would listen and not judge, be objective and do all he could to help. She had to trust somebody, not that she trusted anyone but well, he did seem different.

'That's quite a story. Where does Ashar live?'

'Manchester. He runs a kebab shop. But he visits me a lot.'

'Would it be possible to meet him?'

'He'll be down at the weekend. He wants to move here but we're not sure if this will help get Basma back. What do you think?'

He didn't think anything right then, needed time to get his head round the facts, talk to people who would know a lot more than he did. Meet Ashar.

'Look Serena, I'll give you my number.' He pulled a card from his pocket. 'Here's my home number and mobile. When you know for sure that he's coming, give me a bell and I'll arrange to visit you both. In the meantime I'll ask one or two people I know. Is that OK?'

She nodded.

'Good. Let's go back and see Thelma.' He paused. 'Thanks for coming. Believe me, I will do everything I can to help.'

'Thanks for listening anyway.'

He smiled as they got up.

After locking up, he drove home in deep contemplation. Dawn Adams was the key, she had advised and helped him when he was setting up the mobile catering van. She was one of Tracey's contacts and had put them in touch. He had met with her and Bob Planter at social services to discuss his plans and ensure the council would be supportive. Bob had helped him to buy the catering van and later to sell it when he moved to the rented shop where the centre had been established. He would ring her in the morning.

When they were home, Doug walked into the kitchen. Ruby

sniffed her empty bowl, looking at him hopefully.

'Don't look at me like that, you got plenty of scraps at the centre. This is a new one kidda, how do we help with this one? Guess we'd better get some kip and start in the morning.'

He got a drink of water, switched the light off and went upstairs. Soon they were both asleep on the bed.

They were up bright and early, Ruby eating her breakfast as Doug thoughtfully leaned against the worktop drinking coffee. He took the mug into his study and went through his telephone cards. Been a long time but she must be here, somewhere. Was she filed under A for Adams or D for Dawn? Here we are, D for Dawn.

A voice he did not recognise answered. 'Good morning, children's services.'

'Can I speak to Dawn, please. It's Doug Spencer.'

There was a brief pause and to his relief he heard Dawn's voice. He pictured her in his mind. About fifty, small with a kindly face and probably dressed in something definitely not Gucci which lifelessly draped her ample form like a sack.

'Hi Dawn, Doug Spencer here. Yes, it's been a while. How you doing, or shouldn't I ask!' He waited for the expected reply. 'OK, I won't ask. Look, if you've got a few minutes I'd like to run something past you.'

He explained the basics of Serena's case. When he had finished there was a pause on the line.

'I know this case Doug, it isn't one of mine but I know it. You need to be very careful. I can't say too much but for goodness sake don't get dragged in. It's very complicated.'

'I see that. What if Selena gives her permission for you to talk to me? That would cover any confidentiality issues.'

The line went dead for a moment.

'I suppose that would be OK, as long as she gives it in writing for our records.'

'Right, I'll ask her. Be in touch.'

Dawn slowly put the 'phone down, her face an expression of concern.

Doug looked at his lists. He had made notes about what he had done and what needed doing. He pulled an empty folder from a desk drawer and wrote on the dividers. One for Wally, one for Serena. One for food bank. He gathered his notes together and punched holes in them. Then he shuffled through the lists.

'This is getting bigger than we thought kidda,' he mumbled to Ruby who lay sprawled at his feet chewing on a Dentastix. 'Time for a chat with Sally.'

He put the lists in the relevant dividers. Sally was at work and answered quickly. He stopped filing.

'Morning. How you doing? Me? Sinking in paperwork to be honest, trying to keep up to date.'

She sensed he needed encouragement, to talk things through.

'OK, why don't you come to my place for lunch. Tell you what, pick me up in half an hour, how's that?'

'Great, see you then.'

Ruby followed him into the hall where he collected his coat and scarf.

'We've got time for a quick walk before we get in the car,' he offered as he closed the front door. The magic word, almost as good as food. Her tail wagged in acceptance.

Half an hour later they pulled up outside the MP's office.

Sally put their plates together as she looked at him across the table.

'That was a delicious cheese omelette, thanks,' as he raised his teacup in salute.

'Thank you kind sir. Now, down to business.'

He told her about Serena and her predicament. She let him offload in silence, then felt he wanted, needed her comments.

'It's uncharted water, well at least for us.'

He laughed. 'You mean the impossible can be done at once, miracles take a little longer!'

'Something like that. Look, you need someone independent who knows the system, who can give professional advice.'

'And you know just the person.' There was a tinge of hope in his tone.

'You won't get advice from Dawn because she is bound by confidentiality.'

'So?'

'So I do know a professional, a man who is a consultant child care social worker. If you like, I can arrange a meeting.'

He mulled over her offer. How did she know this man? Would he have the answers?

She read his mind. 'Peter found him when one of his constituents was having problems seeing his son. Long story but he was very helpful. His name is John Brockbank. I've got his number at the office. In fact I'm sure Peter would like to be involved as it is one of his constituents.'

Doug finished his tea and she poured another cup. He thought of the Beatles' song *My Life*.

Though I know I'll never lose affection
For people and things that went before
I know I'll often stop and think about them
In my life I love you more.

How could he love her more than Mary? Love is transient, it moves on. To other dimensions, other people. He did often stop and think about Mary but had come to accept that she was gone. She would want him to love again. Perhaps he loved Sally in a different way. Not more but not less. Just differently.

'I love you, Sally.'

'I know. Me too. You I mean, not me.'

They laughed. It was all so natural.

'OK, let's do it. I'm way out of my depth and need help.'

She guessed that 'way out of my depth' did not refer to their relationship. She had loved him from the moment they first met at the office, it just got deeper and deeper. She too was out of her depth but not in a scary way. It all seemed pre-ordained, meant to be.

Sally had set up a meeting with Peter at the office. As Doug explained the background, Peter was very interested and sat reflecting on what he had been told.

'Do you think Serena would talk to me, want me involved?'

'I can only ask. I'm sure she wants as many big guns as possible, she faces a pretty uphill task by the looks of it.'

There was a knock on the door and Sally entered with a tall, slim, bespectacled man in his late forties.

'Mr Brockbank's here, Peter.' She turned to their guest. 'You know Peter and this is Doug Spencer.' They all shook hands and Sally withdrew discreetly to make coffee.

'John, good to see you again. We need your advice again please.'

John spread his hands. 'Of course, whatever I can offer, Peter.'

'Thanks. Doug, perhaps you would begin.'

Doug was happy when Sally re-appeared with a tray and smiled at her.

'Perhaps you would stay and take notes please, Sally.'

Doug's smile grew wider. He gave the facts as Serena had related them.

'Well, not an unusual situation unfortunately, but it has disquieting features. Let me explain.'

He counted off on his fingers as Sally handed round the cups, then sat down with her notebook.

'One, the Asian factor. Social services in Maidenbury may not be used to working with Muslim families and may have preconceived ideas.

Two, they would need to meet Ashar as soon as possible and be convinced of his sincerity and capability as a father, his experience of childcare.

Three, they would need to assess his capabilities as a father, if he agrees. An assessment would need to be completed of Serena and Ashar's relationship and their joint ability to meet the child's needs. Or separately.'

He paused for a sip of coffee, then continued.

'Four, we have Serena's background. Children already in care and a new untested relationship. How did they get involved? A prostitute and an Asian kebab shop manager.'

'Ex-prostitute,' Doug stressed.

'Yes, but was she doing business when they met? There are many factors that need thorough examination and it will take time. Assuming they both fully co-operate.'

Peter put his cup down. 'What about an investigation separate from social services, would that speed things up?'

'I'm not sure how the family court here would view such a report. The child is already in care so she must have a guardian.'

He studied their bemused expressions.

'Right. Let me explain. A guardian is short for guardian ad litem which is a term used in law to refer to the appointment by a court of one party to act in legal proceedings on behalf of another party. Such as a child or an incapacitated adult, who is deemed incapable of representing them self. In other words, in this case a guardian looks after the child's interests, appoints a solicitor, examines the local authority's case and makes a recommendation to the court.'

Silence.

Doug broke it, choosing his words carefully. 'So this guardian already exists and they are the kingpin.'

'In a nutshell, yes. Do we know who the guardian is?' He looked at their blank expressions. 'OK, I can find out. I know it sounds complicated and long-winded but look at it this way. The judge deciding whether the child should remain in care or go home has many considerations. The welfare of the child is paramount. They listen to all the evidence and read reports. They don't know the parent or parents, or the child.'

Doug and Peter looked at each other, the enormity of the situation beginning to dawn. John continued.

'The courts rely on expert witnesses; the guardian, medical experts, possibly a child psychologist. Then they have to make a decision on a child's life, their future. Guided by the guardian's report.'

Sally looked at Doug, saw his confused expression. She could see him trying to process each layer of information as it developed, trying to absorb and make sense of it all. John held up his hand.

'First things first. You Doug need to meet Ashar. I need to find out who the guardian is and what assessments are planned. Then we go from there.'

Sounded simple. They asked questions, received answers which formulated more questions.

Peter rose. 'Thanks for coming, John. I'm sure we all need to get our heads round what you said. Let's keep in touch.'

Sally showed him out as Peter and Doug stared at each other in puzzled silence.

Chapter Seven

Serena rung just after he got back from an evening at the centre. Ashar would be staying at her place on Friday evening for the weekend, after attending Friday prayers at his local mosque. As Doug replaced the receiver he swung round in his chair. He had been expecting her call and wanted to know more, to dig further into the minefield. People like John Brockbank knew how to negotiate the landmines of child social care, but there would always be things that can go wrong. Especially in this case with many unusual factors. Gosh man, you're even starting to use the terminology! This isn't a case, it is a human tragedy. An explosion waiting to happen.

Saturday morning was arranged, about eleven. Doug thought back on his knowledge of Islam. He had taken an interest, as he had in all religions. He understood the basic articles of Islamic faith: belief in the oneness of Allah, belief in the prophets and in the guidance that they bequeathed, belief in the angels, belief in the books, belief in the Day of Judgment, and belief in fate. And that Muslims believe that Jesus was a prophet of God and was born to a virgin (Mary). He always considered that last point to be noteworthy; he believed in the virgin birth as the son of God, the Messiah. Muslims believe that too, well not the Messiah but a prophet. The holy books include the Quran (given to Muhammad), the Torah (given to Moses), the Gospel (given to Jesus), the Psalms (given to David) and the Scrolls (given to Abraham).

His thoughts turned to Serena. What belief, if any, did she follow? Did she intend converting to Islam? What he didn't know was that when they were in the chapel, she almost asked him to pray for her but felt embarrassed, small, insignificant.

Saturday morning arrived. He had checked with Serena when she rang that it was OK to take Ruby. He had told Thelma the evening before that he was going to meet Ashar. As he drove to the town he felt depressed. The derelict buildings didn't help, the faces of hopelessness they passed. Ruby looked out of the window, glad she wouldn't have to come face to face with the angry snouts of the stray dogs roaming the streets for food, fighting and growling.

The lift was working, a positive omen. Ashar opened the door with a smile. He looked homely in a jumper and jeans, making him look younger than his mid-fifties. His dark skin and hair confirmed his Asian heritage. He welcomed Doug in perfect English with only a hint of a Pakistani accent, shook hands warmly.

Serena hovered in the background but he brought her

forward to greet them. He seemed relaxed, she was clearly nervous. Doug noticed that the lounge was tidy, looked and smelled fresh.

'Please sit down sir, can I get you a drink?'

'I'd love a cup of tea thank you. And my name's Doug, please.'

'Of course Doug. I'm sure your dog would like a biscuit, if that's OK.'

Doug nodded.

Ashar didn't send Serena into the kitchen, going himself and appearing with mugs of tea and a plate of biscuits. He handed mugs to Doug and Serena, broke a biscuit and gave it to Ruby who was on her best behaviour.

They sat in silence, drinking and smiling. Doug hadn't known what to expect but they had got off to a good start.

'Serena has told me about you and that you want to help us. Well, we need all the help we can get Doug. The odds seem to be stacked against us.'

That was an understatement. May as well come straight to the point.

'Your individual circumstances are challenging to the authorities, that's true. Anxiety about the unknown I suppose. But yes, I would like to help if I can. Maybe you could tell me a bit about yourself if you would Ashar, help me to get a better picture.'

Ashar nodded. He glanced at Serena as if to get her agreement. When she smiled, he began. He was born in Pakistan and his parents brought him and his younger sister to England in 1974. His father was a paediatrician and worked at the Pendlebury Children's Hospital in Salford. His mother was a midwife, a career his sister also chose and she worked at a Salford hospital. His parents were now dead but his sister Aiza was married and lived in Manchester with her husband and two boys.

He paused. 'I'm afraid I'm not academically gifted so I have worked in catering all my life.'

'Ah, that's where the kebab shop comes in'.

'Indeed. An honest living though.'

'You never married?'

'No sir, I mean Doug, sorry. I suppose I never found the right girl.' He smiled at Serena. 'Until now that is.'

Doug was trying to fit the jigsaw pieces into place in his mind but some wouldn't fit. He didn't like to ask about Serena's profession, hoping Ashar would get round to that. He waited, but either the other didn't want to go down that road or it wasn't important to him. Or he didn't know.

'So how did you meet?

Serena had come into the shop for a kebab and seemed rather unsteady on her feet. He had given her a kebab and coffee, which she consumed in the shop and was steadier. They talked and she hung around until closing time. They went for a walk and she stayed at his flat above the premises for a few weeks. Then she suddenly disappeared but then rung him one day, told him she was living in Maidenbury.

This man must be naïve or the best liar he had ever met. When he glanced at the imploring look in Serena's eyes he realised the truth. Ashar had no idea of her background; the business side, the drinking, the children taken into care.

Doug got up, thanked him for his openness and quickly made an exit, saying he was late for another visit and would be in touch. He had to think all this through carefully. He did have another visit planned, he had told Thelma the evening before of his visit and that he would call in afterwards. He couldn't, he needed air, needed someone to talk to who would listen, help him make some sense of it all.

She was soft and warm, an oasis in his crazy world. He lay on her breast on the couch in the cottage lounge with eyes closed. He didn't want to open them because then all the scary, cold darkness would flood back in. He felt out of his depth but safe here as she soothingly stroked his hair.

'Am I insane?'

She pulled her head back in surprise and looked down at him.

'No, I don't think so. I mean not to me. What makes you say that?'

'It just feels that way sometimes.'

'No darling, you're not insane. Some of the situations you get into are, life is insane.'

'Am I a coward then?'

'No! That's one thing you're definitely not! What's brought all this on?'

'My life was safe, secure, boring even. I followed the rules, played the game. Then it was all over. I retired.'

'Look at it another way. You entered a new phase, part two. Very different but it took guts to go through that door.'

She always said the right thing, what he wanted, needed to hear. He felt like he was dreaming. The nightmare of loneliness was over, but oh, he was in a world of nightmares, that's for sure, but other people's nightmares. He could help them face their darkness, try to shine some light but only if light shone in his own world.

He opened his eyes and looked up into hers.

'Will you marry me?'

She was surprised at his timing but had no hesitation. She hugged him. 'Yes darling, if you're sure that is what you want.'

'I'm sure.'

They lay in silence. It was a long while before she spoke.

'I've been thinking. Why don't we pop over and collect your car. Right now, traffic shouldn't be too bad on a Saturday and we'll be back in good time for the evening meeting.' Adding as she read his mind, 'I'll drive the estate back.'

He kissed her lips, a celebration of a good decision.

'I don't deserve you.'

'We deserve each other. Come on, I'll get my coat.'

As they went into the hall Ruby followed. She didn't know what was going on but sensed the happiness in the air as she watched them go arm in arm to the car.

Chapter Eight

'Mr Arnold will see you now,' said the receptionist. Ashar followed her into the Manchester solicitor's office and heard the door close behind him.

'Mr Khan, please sit down,' said the trendy figure as he read a file on his desk. 'I have reviewed Ms Hampson's file and it doesn't look good.' He tapped the file with emphasis several times. "Not good at all.'

Ashar waited.

'I advise you to break off any relationship you may have with her and go it alone. Look, if you want to apply for custody of your daughter, you stand no chance with Ms Hampson in tow. You may have a slim chance on your own, no guarantee, but if you are the natural father then there is always a chance, depending on how the local authority assess you. You understand?'

Not really. Ashar did not want to break up with her.

'You will need to have a paternity test, that's the first thing. Assuming you are the father, we can prepare your case. If you agree, please sign here.' He pushed a document across the desk.

'Legal aid is still available on a non-means, non-merits tested basis in care proceedings where it is available for the child who is the subject of the proceedings and for parents with parental responsibility for the subject child. Your name is on the birth certificate, yes?'

He wasn't sure whether Serena had put his name on the birth certificate.

'The simplest way forward is to get the birth certificate re-registered with the General Register Office. This requires the mother's agreement. She needs to complete a statutory declaration that you are the child's father. Will she agree? Once completed, you will duly acquire parental responsibility.'

He pondered all this information.

'With parental responsibility we can begin a custody application. One more thing Mr Khan, you need to get the mother's agreement before you break up with her. She is unlikely to be forthcoming if she knows, even suspects, that you will leave her. Understand?'

Ashar said he needed to think carefully about what he had been told. His head was spinning. He would be in touch as soon as possible. The younger man nodded, gave him a business card, put the folder on a pile on his desk and pulled another from a pile on the other side.

Ashar left. What he did not know was that Serena was already two steps ahead of him. She anticipated he would want custody and might get it. If he did, then she could move in with them. Social services could be kept in the dark, what they didn't know wouldn't hurt them, or her. She did not want to go back to Manchester though, too many bad memories.

Doug sat in the clickie room without clicking, much to Ruby's delight. Maybe he should call it the thinking room. It wasn't exactly a study, well not the size and impressiveness of the ones he had had as a vicar. But it was his, owned and paid for with the money Mary had left him. The residue of her legacy had enabled him to provide for the rent at the centre and evening meals, topped up from his clergy pension and the generosity of a few remaining businesses in the town.

Luck of the draw some would say, you pays your money and you takes your chances. Depends on the hand you get dealt. He thought about Wally and Serena. The cards they were dealt seemed so unfair, how can a life be made out of such a bum deal?

He had been dealt a good hand. Gone to university to study theology, met Mary as a curate, got married, had children. Lived a happy life. Happy yes, from a family point of view, not career-wise. When he retired he had started writing a book about his life as he promised Mary he would, but the more he wrote the more it became a journey into missed opportunities and disillusionment. The more he delved, the more bitter it seemed.

Being a vicar, following the rules and playing the game. Doing what was expected, not rocking the boat. Paperwork, always available, a pillar of society. At the end bitterly questioning the system he had been trapped in. The book had developed into bitterness and anger, made him ask if he was taking out his anger and pain about Mary's passing. It certainly did not become the sort of book Mary had hoped for, a manuscript supporting the system. When he started the centre, met Tracey, he had pressed the delete key.

∝

His pain had subsided, never went away but melted into a kind of acceptance. Time to move on. Now he felt he was doing what he was meant to do, though could he have done it without the background of being a 'normal' vicar? Possibly.

He would never forget the evening at the centre in the early days as he was helping to clear away before the choir started, with Thelma as lead singer, when a group at one of the larger tables who had been gesticulating and talking loudly in each other's face, got to their feet. This group started shouting, well tried to sing *He's a jolly good fellow* and soon the whole room was on its feet joining in. That was the moment when a retired nonentity was re-born into the much loved Rev Doug, non-denominational pastor of a most unusual flock.

Now a food bank was on the cards. And two major headaches had surfaced, Wally and Ashar. There would be others too, that was the nature of reality. Many shy away. Some embrace the brutal hand dealt to others with their time and talents, bring hope, spread love. He considered himself a tiny flickering light in the bosom of humanity, where all good things shine brightly in the warmth of human kindness.

The 'phone rang to interrupt his thoughts. It was Bob Planter.

'Sorry Doug, prepare yourself for bad news, very bad news. I don't quite know how to tell you this, I just found out. I'm afraid Wally hung himself in his cell this morning.'

Doug's breath froze. He wanted to ask how but that was irrelevant. He couldn't speak.

'You still there, Doug?'

He was but his mind was numb. Slowly he started to put down the receiver, then asked 'Does Thelma know?'

'Not yet. I was hoping you would tell her.'

'I'll go now.' He replaced the receiver, leaning back in his chair which creaked reassuringly.

His fist smashed the desktop with a deafening crash. Damn. Damn, damn, damn! He burst into tears.

Funeral visits were part of his trade. Usually to strangers, occasionally to friends and acquaintances. Over the years he had developed a liturgy for such visits with suitable words and phrases depending on the level of faith of the grieving. Level of faith, how do you gauge that. The usual response to his query about how religious they wanted the service to be was not at all, no prayers. He had often thought of suggesting a humanist funeral but thought that impolite and insensitive. Many want a man or woman of the cloth to legitimise the proceedings.

What would Thelma expect? What would she need? Love, understanding, an answer to her question, why. That would be her main question to which he didn't have the answer. Why.

A young man, just a kid, had killed himself in a place where he was supposed to be secure, put there by a system that ground justice out of chaos, to prevent chaos.

He had to put his thoughts aside and concentrate on her. He was in unknown territory, well-trodden, not precise. It seemed to him that their whole life had been misleading and twisted, two kids trying to make sense out of the nonsensical.

He rang Sally, needed to hear her voice. She gasped at the news.

'Oh no. How could that happen?'

'Don't know, I suppose he wanted to do it and found a way.' He paused. 'I failed him Sally, I failed them both.' His voice was flat, matter of fact.

'They were failed but not by you my darling, never by you.'

'I need to see Thelma this morning, before she finds out from someone else. That's the least I can do.'

'Would you like me to come with you?'

'No, thanks. I just needed to hear your voice. Talk later.'

'Ring me Doug, anytime. I'll be praying for you both. I love you.'

That was what he needed to hear. He felt her tenderly blow him a kiss.

✝

Thelma would be at work. He found the supermarket number and rang the manager. Joan was a good supporter of the centre and had offered to help with the food bank.

'Joan, I need to come and see Thelma urgently. I can't go into detail but it is very urgent.' She agreed without question. He thanked her, said he would be about fifteen minutes and rang off.

✝

As he drove he prepared what he was going to say. Ruby lay on her seat. She sensed something bad was happening, Dad was so down. He patted her head.

'OK, you wait here for me, kidda. Won't be long,' he said as he slowly got out of the car. It would probably be one of the longest periods of his life.

He remembered the first time he met Thelma and Wally. The two figures that appeared in the doorway of the old dilapidated caravan he found by chance whilst walking with Ruby near the lock-up. They stood side by side, arms folded in defiance. Ruby had sniffed ferociously, this was good smells.

'You from the council? We ain't movin,' exclaimed the young man, glaring into Doug's face.

'No, we bloody ain't,' echoed the girl.

Doug was taken aback. He had reassured them that he was not from the council and saw their bodies relax. They had put their hands in the pockets of their dirty jeans. They looked like two peas in a pod, dirty pullovers and heavy boots. This old caravan was clearly their residence.

Introducing himself as a visitor to the area out for a walk, they started to talk. Rapidly, with a childlike naivety, often cutting over each other in their need to talk.

He wiped away tears. Happy memories, sacred memories.

He entered the supermarket and saw Joan by a till.

'I'm afraid I have some bad news for Thelma. Is there somewhere quiet we can talk?'

'Use my office.'

They looked at Thelma on a till down the line. She was so absorbed in her work that she didn't notice Doug enter.

'I'll take over her till.'

Doug waited as Joan spoke with her, then Thelma came towards him with a look of surprise. He put his arm round her shoulder as they walked to the office. He knew it well, having been to see Joan on a number of occasions.

'What's up?' she asked as they walked. 'Come on Doug, tell me. Is it about Wally?'

He sat her in a chair and pulled another beside her.

He took her hands in his, taking a deep breath. He told her the bare facts as gently as he could. Wally was gone.

Seconds ticked away like hours.

"No. You're wrong. It's a lie!'

He only wished it was.

'I wanna see him!'

There would be formalities, he was sure of that but he didn't want to go into detail. Thelma being Thelma wanted facts.

'I wanna see him! Doug, I wanna. When?'

'There will be a police investigation and an inquest.' He paused. 'I think you will be asked to identify the body at the post-mortem.'

'So I get to see him after they cut him up!'

'No, I'm sure there is a room where you can see him.'

'At the knife place! I wanna see him before they cut him up!'

She softened slightly, spoke quietly, imploringly. 'Please Doug, make sure I can do that. Please.'

'I'll do my very best, Thelma. I'm sure it can be arranged.'

After a short pause he added, 'Let me take you home. You can stay at Sally's tonight.'

'Nope, I'm going to carry on as normal. Stay here and go to the centre tonight.'

She was adamant. He knew there was no point trying to change her mind. Probably for the best, keep her mind occupied.

'OK, if that's what you want. Can I tell Joan? And make an announcement at the centre tonight?'

She nodded. 'I'll be there. My friends are there.'

He admired her stoicism but that was Thelma.

'Fine, I'll see you there. Is there anything I can do right now?'

'Pray.'

He was taken aback but not entirely surprised. Again, that was Thelma.

'Of course I will. I'm so very sorry Thelma, I really am.' He squeezed her hands.

'I know. So am I.'

With that she got up and left the office. Doug hurriedly followed to catch Joan so she knew what was happening. She would be supportive and keep an eye on her.

He sat in the car and stared out of the windscreen. What a mess. He had someone to go to, someone anxiously waiting. Poor Thelma was all alone in the world.

As soon as he entered, Sally hugged him. She didn't care who looked through the office window, this was her man and he needed her. It was a massive hug which almost took his breath away.

She drew him to a chair and sat next to him, stroking his hand. 'Well?'

'She seems OK, hard to tell. Down to earth, solid. Wants to know when she can see him.'

'Shouldn't take that long, surely?'

He shrugged. 'Could be months, with a police investigation and post-mortem. And they weren't married so I don't know how she stands legally.'

'Come round tonight, you look like you need some comfort.'

'Will you come to the centre first, Thelma said she'll be there.'

'Of course. She's quite a girl, carrying on as usual. I suppose she needs to keep busy to take her mind off things.'

'Exactly.' He looked at his watch. 'I'd better get to the centre, see how things are going. I'm doing an announcement about Wally, so need to think about that. See you there.'

He kissed her. The world seemed to go away, if only for a moment.

Chapter Nine

As he opened up, Doug stopped in the doorway. He felt Wally's spirit present; the laughter, the jokes, looking for people who might need his help, being a large, warm, welcoming part of the fellowship. He couldn't believe that he would never walk through that door again, bouncing around with his infectious energy. His life had been difficult but it had improved when Thelma and Wally moved here. Becoming involved in that petrol station nightmare with good intentions, looking out for a colleague... a cruel twist of fate had snuffed him out like he was a nothing.

Doug stared at a wall. Yes, there. He had a photo of Wally on his own, joking with Thelma standing behind Doug's mobile as she took the photo. He would get it enlarged, printed and framed and put it in the centre of the wall for all to see.

He went into the chapel and sat in front of the altar. The wooden Cross seemed to shine, surrounded by an intense light.

'You work in mysterious ways, Lord. Awful ways.' He closed his eyes, bringing Thelma into his consciousness, then both of them. He sat there for maybe half an hour until he heard helpers arriving. First the cooks, then the minders and musicians. As he went into the hall, Thelma arrived. She looked pale and uncertain as she stood by the door.

He went to her, hugged her limp body and whispered, 'Sure you want to be here?' She nodded. He led her into the chapel and sat her down. He was about to talk about his words to the others after their meal, before the singing, get her agreement, when Sally came in and sat with them. She hugged Thelma, gently took her hands as she looked into her eyes. They sat in respectful silence.

After a few minutes Thelma looked at Sally and said very quietly, 'I'm pregnant.'

The words were like a bomb exploding; a deafening, jarring explosion, a traumatic blinding flash of revelation.

The centre was full and a meal of lamb cutlets with boiled potatoes and cabbage had been consumed, followed by lemon sponge with custard. The mood was happy, the chatting loud. Bad events in each participants' life forgotten in a few moments of warmth and fellowship.

Doug didn't want it to end, he wanted the music that followed to put the crown on the evening, as it did every evening. Tonight was different. He watched Thelma, trying to see if she would be able to sing. Sally was sitting by her side, had offered their love and full support especially in the coming months. She had estimated that Thelma was nearly three months pregnant.

As he walked round, he watched Thelma out of the corner of his eye. She seemed her normal self, chatting and laughing.

He went over and whispered in her ear, 'You OK to sing?' She nodded. 'If you're sure I'll say something now.' Again she nodded.

He clapped his hands loudly. As usual he had to clap a few times, even bang on a table.

'Friends, we're going to sing in a minute, led as ever by the lovely Thelma and the choir and musicians.' He paused for the shouts and banging on tables to subside.

'Tonight I have to announce some very sad news.' He paused, looking round the faces. 'I'm afraid I have to tell you that Wally passed away today.'

The room fell silent. Looks of disbelief were followed by an outpouring of sadness, some anger. Without a word they got up and went to put their arms round Thelma, who started to weep. When there were too many to physically touch her, they hugged those around her. Sally moved away to give room. He waited for a suitable moment, it was a long wait.

'Thank you friends. Thelma would like to sing for you now.'

Slowly they moved away to allow her to go to the front. Without a word she took the microphone, looking at the musicians and singers. They seemed shaken but ready. The room broke into respectful clapping.

She quietly counted one, two, three and broke into her and Wally's favourite hymn *Amazing Grace*. Everyone joined in; tears flowed, arms were raised.

There were a couple of extra hymns that evening, all chosen by Thelma without any rehearsal, it all just flowed.

Doug held Sally's hand as they sang along. When Thelma

had finished a silence fell on the congregation. He went to the front and hugged her, whispered 'Thank you, Wally would be so proud.'

He turned to the gathering and offered a prayer of comfort, hope, thanks for Wally's life and for Thelma. The shouts of *Amen* were sincere, deafening.'

They didn't want to leave but eventually slowly straggled out, talking in quiet tones to each other.

Doug and Sally drove Thelma home and stayed with her. They talked about the baby and their future, trying to take her mind off Wally. She asked when his funeral would be but Doug steered her away from that thought, saying he would let her know as soon as he heard anything but it might take a while. He reminded himself to keep checking with Bob Planter, he would be in the know.

She said she was alright, she had friends and Serena was just down the corridor. Doug was alarmed, thinking was that a good idea? Or would their mutual need be helpful? Better sleep on that one.

It was past midnight when they left, Doug saying as they walked to the lift that she must contact him whenever she felt the need. He would keep in touch. The lift was out of order so he and Sally descended step by step, the air stinking of damp and urine.

They did not speak on the descent as bodies of varying ages were gathered in groups on each floor, joyless and depressed, some worse for wear.

They breathed deeply as they exited the block, needing fresh air but even there the pungent mustiness seemed all around.

'We're going back to my place for the night.'

He nodded. Ruby wagged her tail as they thankfully approached the car.

Doug lay with Sally on his chest. He was mulling over events, trying to put them into perspective. Thelma, the baby, Ashar and Serena and their baby, the food bank, impending marriage.

'You awake?' he whispered.

'Difficult to sleep.'

'Yeah, you can say that again.' He paused. 'Been thinking.'

She looked up.

'Let's get married soon. Soon as possible.'

She raised her head to look at him.

'How soon? I mean you're up to your neck and it doesn't look like easing off any time soon. Mind you, will it ever!'

'Guess not. So better just get on with it.'

'How romantic! There's a lot to plan. Where, ceremony, invites.'

'I'm sure Jim would be delighted to officiate. And we do it at the centre. Invite whoever wants to come, no formal invitations.'

'You'd better talk to your daughters first.'

'Yes. I'll ring Angela in the morning.'

'Won't they think it strange; you talk to them now and again, then suddenly out of the blue invite them to your wedding to a woman they don't even know.'

'I've been thinking about that. They both live near Bristol and it's Angela's birthday next week. She'll be having a get together with Beth. I'll ring Angela and say I'd like to see them, and that I have a surprise.'

'Oh that sounds wonderful! You invite yourself to your eldest daughter's birthday party, then announce you're getting married and by the way, surprise surprise, here's the bride! Very sensitively done, I don't think.'

'Yes, you've got a point.'

'You bet I have!'

'OK, I'll ring Angela and bring her up to speed.'

'How much does she know?'

'Well, I've told her about the centre and that things are developing with the food bank. That's about it really.'

Silence. Sally didn't want to be seen as an interloper; this had to be done tactfully, feelings considered, memories honoured and respected. She was aware that his relationship with his daughters, and grandchildren, was not close but not distant. There for each other but not in each other's pockets. How would they take to his getting marriage again? Would she be accepted?

Doug put down the 'phone and swung from side to side in his office chair. That went well, very well. He had told Angela about Sally and their forthcoming wedding, she and Beth would be delighted to meet her next week. He had known it would be well, that there wouldn't be a problem. Yes!

Ruby looked up at him, knew something good was happening, happy that Dad didn't use that clickie thing much these days. Tap tap tap, very disquieting when a dog is attempting to sleep.

The 'phone rang. 'Doug? I've been trying to reach you. Listen, Ashar's been arrested, he's in court tomorrow. Parental abduction.'

Doug let this information from Bob Planter sink in.

'You mean he has abducted Basma? '

'Right. He visited her at the foster home, took her for a walk and didn't return her. They rang the police. He got picked up at the railway station.'

'Does Serena know?'

"Don't think so. Any chance you could tell her, I'm up to my eyes. Thanks.'

He rang off.

Not good news. Frustration probably. He guessed when a father finds the system exasperatingly slow and stacked against them, the temptation to grasp it into their own hands can be overwhelming. Often without fully thinking through the consequences.

He rang Serena, she was at home. He said he would call round in half an hour.

The lift was in order, that is working but with juddering bumps and a grinding noise. As Doug knocked on her door a man hurriedly made for the stairs. Punter or junk-seller? He checked himself at these slang expressions, conscious that the more he became involved with 'real' life, the more deadpan he became. A year ago such a thought would never have crossed his mind. Nothing seemed to surprise him now. He still cared, more than ever, but tinged with a certain flatness. Maybe self-protection, like putting on waders before plunging into deep water.

Serena opened the door slightly, peering through the gap. On recognising him she opened it fully.

'Have you heard about Ashar and Basma?' he began as they went into the living room. Clearly she had not. He told her what Bob had said as they stood in the middle of the floor.

'Shit! The bloody fool,' she exclaimed angrily. 'Is she back at the foster home?'

He assured her that would be the case.

'Bastard. That's done it, he's blown any chance now. We'll never get her back.'

Her mind churned scenarios. He had played right into their hands. Screwed it up for both of them. She had little or no chance, with him there had been a possibility. Slim but possible. Now...

'That's it then. Goodbye Basma.'

Doug didn't want to appear confident about a subject of which he had little knowledge, so he chose his words carefully.

'Not necessarily. OK, he's made a mistake but an understandable one. It could be seen as his rather rash attempt to look after his daughter. Show he cares.'

She thought about it. Yeah, that's true. Maybe. Her encounters with social services flashed through her mind. She had eventually accepted that they had Basma's welfare at heart, but so had she as the mother. Of four children. Now five. Four gone forever.

'I'm trying, I've done everything they asked. I'm not going to get Basma back on my own though. The deck's stacked against me but he has, had, a chance.'

'And may still have. Look, I'll make some enquiries, talk to some people. OK?'

'OK.' She didn't sound convinced.

The lift doors creaked open, like the gates of hell he thought as he and Ruby dubiously crossed the gap of no return, displaying the deep unfathomable darkness below the swaying metal cage.

Peter Barker's office. Doug was glad to get out of the torrential rain as he rushed through the front door, loosely shaking his coat from the front as Ruby shook herself. As Sally took his coat she whispered 'Tracey's here too. I'll stay here, unless Peter wants me to join in.'

She knocked and opened the door to reveal Tracey sitting in front of the desk, both drinking coffee. She smiled as he entered, Peter waving to a chair next to her.

'Bad day Doug, bad days all round it seems,' Peter said as Doug sat down.

'Yes.' He glanced at Tracey. 'Let's hope we can sort things out.'

Then it struck him that she might take that the wrong way.

'I've invited Tracey as I think we need some press coverage, Doug. Sally's given me some details, please fill in the gaps. Oh sorry, coffee?'

Doug shook his head. 'No thanks. OK, here goes.'

He continued from where he knew Peter had last been involved. As he spoke, Peter nodded and made notes, looking up occasionally. Tracey was scribbling hard.

When Doug had finished, Peter sighed heavily.

'Thanks Doug. What a tragedy. I see it like this. Serena and Ashar. Well, let's hope the court will give Ashar a probation order, he needs advice and help. And Families Need Fathers must be contacted, they can be very helpful. I've been in touch again with John Brockbank, put him in the picture. He says it will be an uphill struggle but Ashar still has a chance of gaining custody. The child's guardian seems to be on his side and the mother agrees to his name going on the birth certificate so he will have parental responsibility.'

Tracey looked up. 'What about Wally? How can we try to clear his name when he didn't even go for trial?'

'Yes, that's true. He wasn't convicted and innocent until proven guilty. What about starting a campaign for justice, Tracey?'

She nodded and made notes.

Doug admired Tracey, her professionalism and sound judgement. Their relationship was water under the bridge, they had moved on. No matter how he tried, when he pictured Tracey he saw betrayal. Could he trust her? Once bitten…

He owed it to her to tell her that he was marrying Sally. After this meeting would be a good time?

The rain was in remission as he followed her into the street. As he passed Sally's desk he mimed 'Going to tell her' but her raised eyebrows indicated she did not understand. How many women would simply smile when you walk past them with an ex, Doug wondered? Not many.

Tracey turned to him when they were outside.

'Well, it all seems to be getting sorted. Happy?'

Not really. Happy about how things are working out, not happy about having to tell you, Tracey. OK, here goes.

'Have you got a minute, or do you have to dash off?'

'I've got a few minutes,' her voice questioning.

'Let's have a coffee.' He led her to a café as they walked in silence.

Inside he looked round, glad it was almost empty. They sat at a corner table.

'Coffee?' She nodded and he went to the counter. She looked at his back as he ordered. What did he want to talk about? She was still pondering when he returned.

'Won't be long before this place closes too, I guess,' he said as he put the cups on the table.

Not doing very well Doug, not well at all. Get on with it. He stirred his coffee, looking at the froth. Suddenly he looked up.

'Tracey, I've got something to tell you. I'm, eh, getting married.'

She stopped stirring. 'Oh.'

Was she surprised? Upset? He stared into her eyes, trying to read some expression, any expression. Nothing.

'Yes. To Sally.'

Still no reaction. He felt under the table for Ruby. There she was.

Silence. She seemed to be searching his face.

'We're good friends Tracey, been through a lot together. Thought you should be the first to know.' He tried to smile.

At last she spoke. 'Well, that's a surprise. I hope you'll both be very happy.'

She sounded sincere. Was it alright then, did he have her blessing? He couldn't read her mind, probably a good job. If he had, he would have witnessed her turmoil, deep sadness that a line was being drawn in the sand. So far, no further.

She got up. 'Thank you for telling me. I'd better get off now, things to do.'

He rose. 'Still friends?' He held out his hand. Hers was warm, the hand he knew so well.

'Still friends.' Adding with a fleeting smile, 'Bye Doug. Bye Ruby.' She patted her, quickly turning for the door to hide her tears.

He sat down. That was awful. Wasn't there enough pain around without inflicting more...

Chapter Ten

It was early as they were sped along the M4 bound for Redland, Bristol. Dawn had broken, looked like a bright day for a change. Ruby was asleep on the back seat. Sally tried to appear relaxed, her mind churning at the thought of meeting Angela and Beth. Doug understood the mixture of happiness and apprehension she must be feeling. He squeezed her hand, glancing across with a supportive smile. She responded with a smile.

He looked at a signpost as they left the motorway. Strange, he hadn't been here that many times but felt like he knew the way. If he was honest, he was nervous too. He had no doubt that Sally would be warmly received, his girls were kind and accepting. No problem there. So why did he feel slightly apprehensive? No, not apprehensive, more nervous tension. He wanted to arrive early so they could talk with the girls whilst his grandchildren were at school.

Seeing a roadside café, he pulled into the car park. Time for a break, time to kill. As he switched off the ignition he looked at his watch.

'We made better time than planned. Fancy some breakfast?'

'Why not. What time did you say we'd arrive?'

'About nine-thirty, when they get back from the school run. Beth will go straight to Angela's.'

They entered and sat at a table. The place was deserted apart from one or two truckers.

'Fancy a full breakfast? I'm hungry.'

'Oh no thanks, coffee and toast is fine.'

'Right.' He stood up, paused and sat down again.

'You OK?' he asked.

'Yes, I think so. Bit nervous to be honest.'

'Me too, don't know why though.' He hesitated. 'Funny thing, being a parent. One minute you're together all the time, then you go separate ways. Guess that's letting go. The strength of the relationship is in future contact.' He sighed, looking at the table.

'It is what it is Doug. Things happen. Don't beat yourself up.'

He forced a smile. 'You're right. Can't wind the clock back.'

She took his hand. 'Hey, don't go all morbid on me! Come on, let's eat. Ruby's waiting.'

'She's always waiting for food,' he laughed as he headed for the counter.

He returned carrying a tray laden with a full English, a large plate of toast and butter and two coffees.

'Got extra toast. I want some with my breakfast and some with marmalade afterwards.'

'Greedy!'

'No, just hungry. Guess who'll scoff as much toast as she can get.' Ruby was already sniffing the air.

They ate in thoughtful silence. Now and again they looked at each other, started to speak then thought better. What was there left to say?

When they had finished, Doug got more coffee. Ruby looked hopeful. 'That's your lot for now. You can have your breakfast at Angela's.' He had put a tin of dog food in the car.

Eventually they were on their way again. A kind of hush enveloped the car.

⧸⧸

They arrived at the neat, modern three-bedroomed semi-detached, at the head of a cul-de-sac. Beth lived a short walk away so there was only one car in the driveway.

Doug stopped the car on the road outside. They saw a figure at the front window, looking out.

'That's Angela.' He stroked her hand and opened his door. 'Ready?'

'Ready.'

Angela opened the front door and hugged her father, who introduced Sally. Angela did not hesitate to give her a lingering hug of acceptance. Sally looked at Doug whilst being hugged, his expression was 'Told you so!'

'Come on Beth, look who's here,' Angela called.

Beth appeared from the back of the hall and repeated the embraces. She seemed more reticent but no less sincere. Doug had explained earlier that Angela is the outgoing one, her sister a little more reserved.

Angela led them into the lounge, holding Sally's hand. Beth

94

linked her father's arm. Sally thought how alike they were, twins almost with their fair hair and blue eyes. They even dressed in a similar fashion; light-coloured blouses and slacks. Sally knew their ages; thirty-one and twenty-eight.

'What a lovely suite,' Sally commented as they sat down.

'It's microsuede,' Doug said with humour. 'Manmade fabric. They're both vegan.'

'Don't get on that subject again, thank you Dad,' Angela scolded. 'Boring.'

She smiled at Sally. 'You must be ready for a drink, tea or coffee?'

When all orders had been taken, she left. The room went quiet. Sally looked briefly at Doug, then spoke to Beth.

'What time will the children be home from school? I can't wait to meet them.'

'Oh, about three-thirty. We walk to pick them up.'

'That's nice. Can we join you?'

Beth was about to reply in the affirmative when her father interjected.

'Ah, the monsters. You'll be sorry meeting them, they'll run you ragged.'

Angela entered with a tray.

'Sorry Angela, I should have offered to help. Can I do anything?' Sally was a little embarrassed.

'Yes, you can sit still and enjoy your coffee.' They all laughed.

'Let me get this right. Mark is eight, Jane five and Sarah three.'

'Sarah's mine,' Beth offered, feeling she should say something.

'Wonderful!'

'Ha, bet you won't be saying that on the way home. Sarah's the worst.'

They all made faces at him.

'Will we meet your partners?' Sally asked.

There was a lull which caused her some concern. Had she said the wrong thing? Eventually, Angela spoke.

'Well, you can meet Joe, depends on what time you want to leave and what time he finishes work.' She glanced at Beth. 'Adrian may be a problem. Actually, Adrian IS a problem. They've split.'

'Oh, I'm sorry, I didn't mean to… well, I mean.' Sally was taken aback, Doug hadn't mentioned any no-go areas.' She looked imploringly at him. He turned to his younger daughter.

'I knew you are having some difficulties Beth, has it got worse?'

'He's gone.'

Sally wanted the floor to swallow her up. She braced herself. 'I'm sorry if I've, well, you know.'

Angela jumped in. 'The bastard has run off with an old school friend. Good riddance.'

'I'm so sorry Beth. Is there anything I can do?' Doug's voice was full of concern as he went over and hugged her. She clung to him, shaking her head.

'Happy families, if it's not one thing it's another,' said Angela, trying to lighten the mood. 'Let's change the subject shall we.'

Easier said than done. An uncomfortable pause fell over the conversation.

'I remember a park somewhere near. Shall we go for a walk, then get lunch, my treat.' Doug's endeavour to raise the atmosphere was gratefully accepted, the sighs of relief were almost palpable.

They walked, Doug and Beth talked. Beth was getting a

divorce, matters had come to a head and that was the only option. She would keep the house, she and Sarah could manage the mortgage with her PA job. Adrian had agreed to pay maintenance, his computer engineer business was growing. His mother would help with childcare.

Doug felt guilty. He had been so engrossed in sorting out his own life that he had neglected his duty as a father. He was so thankful that he was not alone, Sally would talk it all through with him, be supportive.

Mary, oh Mary, you wouldn't have let the family get into this state. You'd have been there; supporting Beth, caring for Sarah. Offering your precious advice, would simply have been there, loving and caring without question. That chapter's gone, floated into eternity. It's the here and now, coping with the present.

He watched Ruby scampering around, sniffing the other dogs, not a care in the world. Food, walkies, sleep. As long as she had love and attention in her daily mix, life was very good.

Sally walked with Angela, they seemed to be getting on well. Doug suspected they were discussing him, the father and partner. Doug whose star is rising. From loneliness and despair to a sense of purpose, new love. They walked quite a way behind the other two, conversations were detached yet curiously intertwined.

They went back to Angela's and had a drink. Doug gave Ruby her breakfast. The atmosphere was relaxed, the conversation light-hearted. They chatted as though they had known each other for a long time. The girls asked about the centre and how it was progressing. Doug mentioned the problems but did not go into detail, concentrating on the developing food bank. They thought this an excellent idea, need everywhere, even in their own reasonably affluent area. Angela spoke of her role as a community midwife, her concerns about the profession and the NHS generally. That provoked much debate for over half an hour.

They walked to a local pub for lunch, a favourite of the girls because it served vegan food. After they had ordered Angela went to the ladies' room, Sally following a few minutes later. Angela was washing her hands when Sally entered.

'I just want to say how happy I am that we came, Angela. It's lovely to meet you both at last.'

'Yes, we've broken the ice, haven't we.' She smiled at Sally in the mirror as she dried her hands, adding, 'Dad seems happy.'

'Yes, I believe he is. It must be difficult for you and Beth, losing your Mum and your Dad re-marrying.'

Angela shrugged. 'That's life, it goes on, has to.'

'I suppose so. I do hope we can all be friends.'

'Don't see why not.' She paused. 'As long as Dad's happy, we're happy.'

They were face to face now.

'Good. That sounds fine.'

'I can see you're a bit nervous, no need to be. I have a good feeling about you and your relationship. Hey, we'd better get back or they'll think we've run out the back door. I don't normally do that until after I've eaten.'

They laughed and returned to the lounge bar. The day got better and better, the meal was excellent, though Doug and Sally did not opt for the vegan menu.

The meeting with Doug's grandchildren went well, the children behaved themselves and enjoyed seeing their grandfather and Ruby again.

They were fascinated by Sally and asked if she wanted to be called 'Grandma'. This caused her some consternation but the other adults took the view that if she was happy with that, why not.

Angela commented that Sally didn't look like a Grandma as it was a bit old for her and suggested a little competition to find a suitable name. After hilarious attempts, Gran-Sall was chosen. Then shortened to Gransa.

Joe had been held up at work but Sally said she hoped to meet him another time.

Goodbyes said, Doug, Sally and Ruby headed home. Sally waved until they were out of sight, savouring her last image of them all waving.

'Told you it would be OK, Gransa! How you feeling?'

They were approaching the M4.

'Relieved! They're all so lovely, Doug. You must be very proud.'

'I am. Pity things have taken a nosedive for Beth. I need to keep more in touch with her.'

'Yes, she'd appreciate that.'

'Well, back to reality.' He sighed. 'I've made lists.'

'Of course you have. What are these new lists about?'

'Oh, supporting Thelma, trying to help Ashar and Serena. Getting the food bank off the ground. And getting married.'

'And your marriage list?' She smiled at him.

'Mmm. Date, guests. Where we live.'

They drove in silence. Where to live. Pros and cons. She wasn't attached to her bungalow but the Pilot was there. That could be sorted. How? If she sold the bungalow and they lived at Doug's, she would need a car to get to work. They could afford that, a small item to add to the lists.

Doug was thinking along similar lines, they both liked the cottage with its quiet location. Should he sell the Pilot? That thought didn't appeal, anyway they wouldn't need the money. They could build a garage, there was enough land at the side. Not a concrete monstrosity but discrete, in keeping with the cottage.

They arrived at the centre and started preparations. No-one else had arrived and as they moved around sorting this and that, they chatted. On Valentine's Day it would be the centre's first anniversary.

'Let's get married on Valentine's Day, that gives us five weeks.'

'Wow, that's quick! Can it be done in such a short time?'

'Don't see why not. I've already checked with Jim and he's ready.'

'Oh, you didn't mention that one!'

'Well I told him we want to get married soon. We do, don't we?'

'You know we do, silly. I suppose it can be done, the date is certainly romantic.'

'And it's the centre's first anniversary. Wouldn't it be fantastic to combine the two.'

She smiled at him. Yes it would, dearest Doug, celebrating two big events in your life. She stroked his cheek.

Chapter Eleven

Doug was humming in the clickie room as he updated various lists. The rain was beating against the window but his mood was definitely upbeat. Ruby wandered backwards and forwards, round and round as she waited impatiently for walkies.

The 'phone rang. He removed his reading glasses as he reached for the receiver. It was Dawn Adams from children's services. He was expecting news about the food bank and wasn't prepared for what she said.

Ashar had obtained parental responsibility for Basma and had applied for weekly access. Their family centre was full and could not accept any more supervised contact sessions. Would Doug be willing to offer supervised contact at the centre? Two hours every Saturday morning. He would not have to leave them unsupervised at any time and would be asked to submit a report on how the sessions progressed.

He thought this through. Didn't seem too complicated, just to be there to keep a watchful eye on things. It would certainly help Ashar in his custody application and Serena must have agreed.

'When will this start, Dawn?'

'If you are agreeable, next Saturday from ten to twelve. The foster mother will drop Basma at the centre and collect her. Ashar will make his own way. I suggest you open up at nine-thirty.'

'Will Serena be there?'

'No. She is still being assessed, separately.'

'OK, I'll do it. Do I need assessing?'

She laughed. 'I think we know all we need to know about you, Doug. You're a pillar of the community!'

As he rang off, Doug thought of his first meeting with Dawn. The crowded offices in a concrete monolith. Dawn had found a small meeting room and introduced herself and Bob Planter, the probation officer. She was such a dumpy figure. Bob was surprisingly clean shaven except for a Pancho Villa moustache which drooped at the corners. Late forties he had guessed, clad in jumper and jeans with glasses which kept sliding onto his broad nose. He may have been a boxer in his youth. It was mainly his ears that told the story of beatings to both sides of the head.

Both had spoken of the social deprivation and petty crime in Maidenbury. Doug had explained that he had seen the town during the day and at night, and did not know which was worse.

They had asked about his background and experience. He was honest about his background, to which they had remained without expression. He was relieved for the absence of raised eyebrows, knowing looks or deep sighs. They seemed to accept him for what he was, a bloody do-gooder. When things had got as bad as they were in the town, any helping hand was welcome.

They were good listeners, adept at making correct assessments and decisions. They did both have that in common he had thought. Mind you, when things are at rock bottom choices are limited. Stay as they are, sink irredeemably into the mire or actually begin slowly to rise.

On a practical level they could advise on health & safety, open doors and assured him of no lack of clients. The homeless would be clambering for help when they found out of his existence.

They had suggested that a mobile catering van would be a good start. To be in a certain place at certain times, become known and trusted. They were available for sale at one or two specialist garages, Bob knew where. The council would do an inspection and grant necessary licences.

Dawn had added that no agency had any spare money. If he wanted to do this, financially he was on his own.

One last point. Do not, under any circumstances hand out money, for your own sake. Keep it to meals and some grocery and toiletry items if and when available.

Seemed like an age ago rather than a year. He was a raw amateur then but they had been very helpful and supportive.

The centre looked clean and tidy as Doug prepared for Ashar and Basma's visit. He cleared a space for them to play, checking there were no dangerous objects in reach. He looked at his watch. Nine-thirty.

Ruby wandered around, doing her check. She wasn't sure what for but Dad was here early so something must be happening. He seemed a bit anxious so she did too.

At nine-fifty Ashar arrived. There had been much legal discussion about his case, whether he should be prosecuted for his abduction of Basma. It was decided that this was a one-off offence and that he did not intend to remove her from the country. In reviewing all the circumstances and reading the probation report, it was considered that he needed help and support and was given a two year probation order. Bob Planter was his probation officer.

He seemed on top form, smiling and chatty while they waited for Basma to arrive. He found Bob very understanding and helpful. He admitted that he had panicked and took Basma on a whim. He wouldn't do it again.

The foster mother was late arriving. At ten-fifteen she strode in without a word of apology. She removed Basma from the baby carrier, then hesitated.

She handed her to Doug, with two bottles. It was clear she did not like Ashar, didn't even acknowledge his presence as he stood with outstretched arms. When Doug had Basma firmly in his arms, she gave him two nappies and instructions not to leave the child alone under any circumstances. If he needed the loo, he should go now before she left. When Doug replied that he was OK, she turned for the door, stating over her shoulder that she would return at twelve sharp. Her whole demeanour screamed that she was highly dissatisfied with the whole arrangement.

When she had stormed out, Ashar looked at Doug with a shrug. He held out his arms and took Basma, stared into her face and gave her a big cuddle, softly murmuring *adorable* in Urdu. Doug was aware that according to Muslim custom, Ashar would have whispered the *Adhan* into the baby's right ear shortly after her birth.

These words include the name of Allah the Creator and is followed by the Declaration of Faith: *There is no deity but Allah; Muhammad is the Messenger of Allah.'*

He also knew from his study of other religions that her scalp hair would have been shaved, traditionally on the seventh day of life, with an equivalent weight in silver given to charity. He didn't doubt that Ashar would have arranged for this ceremony if he possibly could, with someone from a local mosque to perform the Sunnah or head shaving.

He realised the foster mother was probably only used to fostering white, British (nominal Christian?) children, things like shaving Basma's head would have horrified her. He also wondered what Serena thought.

He watched the interaction between father and daughter, pleased to see the love Ashar displayed. He changed her nappy and fed her, asking where he could warm one of the bottles. So far, so good. But how would he go on when asked to complete a parenting course? That would be essential if he wanted custody.

The time passed quickly. When Doug looked at his watch it was almost twelve. He helped Ashar tidy up, commenting that the session had gone well and he looked forward to next Saturday. Ashar had not stopped holding his baby since Doug handed her over and looked more and more downhearted as the minutes ticked by.

At two minutes to twelve, the door opened loudly and in

she strode. Without a word she took Basma and her things and left, ignoring Ashar's thanks and plea 'See you next week.'

Doug pulled up a couple of chairs, indicating to Ashar to sit down. He wanted to use the moment alone to find out more about his circumstances. To his surprise, Ashar was upbeat. The latter smiled as he surveyed Doug, saying he felt sorry for the foster mother because she seemed to be locked into her preconceived perception of Islam. Then he really surprised him when he asked how Doug was doing at the centre, with genuine concern.

Doug told him about how it started and where he hoped it was going, with the possibility of establishing a food bank. The other seemed really interested as he thought for a moment.

'I think I may be able to help you. I have friends in the wholesale food industry who would see it as a duty to help. Muslims are brethren, they never do wrong to each other, they never forgo supporting each other, never abandon their brethren in hardship.'

Doug reflected on the people who come to the centre. He had met one or two regular Muslims but had not given them much additional thought. They were always friendly and grateful, mixed and were accepted. The centre isn't about religion, it assists those in need whatever their colour or creed. Need drew them all together, religion divides. Some want to talk, some don't. Those who need extra support and advice, even practical help, were given it. But the centre always needs all the help it can get.

'That would be great, thank you. I'm in the process of talking to various people and groups who might help us to get the food bank off the ground.'

'Well, I am sure you are more than capable of organising it. But you will need a regular supply of quality goods at reasonable prices. The brothers I know have that, they supply many shops all over the country with halal meat, tinned goods, fresh fruit and vegetables.'

Doug had some understanding of halal, that animals must be alive and healthy at the time of slaughter and all blood is drained from the carcass. During the process, a Muslim will recite a dedication, tasmiya or shahada. He knew that if the animal is treated poorly, or tortured while being slaughtered, the meat is haram, the opposite of halal. Forbidden food substances include alcohol, pork, carrion, the meat of carnivores and animals that died due to illness, injury, stunning, poisoning, or slaughtering not in the name of God.

He had to ask. 'What does Serena make of your belief? Does she understand?' He was surprised by the simple answer.

'Yes, she wants to convert to Islam.'

Well well, that's an interesting conundrum Doug thought. Is she just saying this because it may be what he wants to hear, or is she sincere?

There was no way to sugar coat the pill. 'You do understand that Serena has been assessed and observed several times. The probability is, Ashar that she won't be allowed to keep Basma. Therefore the choices are you, long term fostering and then probably adoption into a Muslim family. Those, as I understand it, are the choices the authorities have to make.'

'I understand. She is my daughter and I want to bring her up.' Ashar's intense gaze did not waiver from Doug's face. It was imploring and sincere.

'I know. So we have to move forward step by step, carefully.'

Ashar nodded. He seemed up for the challenge, knowing he had much to gain and everything to lose.

$\propto$

Lists again. Ruby lay in her place in the clickie room as Dad checked his lists. Ashar was true to his word and several Muslim wholesalers contacted Doug to offer their help for the food bank. They would supply goods at cost, a few at no cost. Islam doesn't differentiate between Muslims and non- Muslims when it comes to charity or helping a person.

As he looked at the list of potential suppliers, he knew a major decision had to be made. Buying food would cost money, even at cost price, He had spoken with Jim several times about his centre which supplied items at specific prices, with vouchers from social services, schools, medical centres and others accepted. This required admin help to keep everything running smoothly.

Doug had sounded out his helpers at the centre and many were willing to assist with the food bank, or knew others who would agree to come on board. He had a separate list for this necessity. His landlord was happy with the rent being paid every month and that there was no trouble at the centre. He had agreed that another of his empty shops could be used rent free to store non-perishable goods, which would be the majority. The council had given their blessing.

He checked the food bank list one more time, putting a line through any remaining items. Ready to go!

$\propto$

The sun was trying to shine through grey clouds as people filed into the centre for the official opening of the food bank. It was already packed. Peter and Sally, Bob Planter and Dawn, Ashar with Serena, the mayor and his wife suitably adorned, helpers, regulars mixed with hopefuls. Pastor Jim was there, as were various representatives from local churches and the mosque. Ruby frolicked round, welcoming known and unknown. Tracey walked round with her camera, tried to find room to take photos.

There was one person missing. Doug looked at the large photo which graced the long side wall. Wally smiled mischievously down on the gathering. The inquest was imminent. His funeral could take place soon afterwards. The campaign to clear his name had gained many supporters, spurred on by Tracey's Chronicle crusade.

Doug weaved his way to the front and held up his hand as Tracey's camera clicked continuously. He had prepared a speech in his head, glancing at Sally as he threaded his way through the crowd. She smiled encouragement as he cleared his throat.

'Good morning ladies and gentlemen, thank you for coming. And welcome to our Lord Mayor and Lady Mayoress for taking the time from your busy schedule. And of course our MP, Peter Barker who always works so hard for us.'

He waited for the applause to subside, thanking all who had made this day possible with their donations, both financial and with offers of regular food supplies. He went on to explain how the food bank would operate, starting today! More applause. From twelve to two each day, those in employment or not could collect non-perishable items and perishable goods when available. He waited for the applause to subside.

'Everyone has a right to eat. A man once said in a book that man does not live by bread alone but by every word that proceeds from the mouth of God. True, but if man does not have bread, how can he or she concentrate on anything? It is a basic necessity of life.'

Deafening applause.

'So from today friends, we rejoice that no-one, no family, man, woman or child in this town will go hungry again!'

He held up his hand and the cheers and whistles died down.

'Thank you. On behalf of all those who will work day in, day out, to make this a great success, I will ask our Lord Mayor to declare this food bank now open!'

He went round the room shaking hands, winking at Sally as he passed her. And thought of Mary who would be so proud, offering a silent prayer of thanks that her estate had helped to make it possible.

∝

A normal day; Doug, Ruby and his mobile were in the clickie room. It rang.

'Morning Doug, Johnny Redmayne the mayor here. I just want to thank you for yesterday. Have you ever thought of becoming a local councillor, we need people like you.'

'Well thank YOU, Mr Mayor. To be honest, I haven't thought about it. I will of course consider it, though.' What else could he reply to such a dubious inquiry!

After chatting about this and that, the line went dead. Politics. Ruby sniffed. Peter Barker is a Labour politician, the local council run by Labour. All doing excellent work in their own way. In his own village the voters were mainly Conservative. Way of the world.

Doug knew instinctively that he was not a politician. What

was he then? No longer a vicar, heaven knows they are divided in their politics. He had read of a bishop who was about to be appointed, had agreed, but his future flock rebelled, saying they did not want him because he did not accept the ordination of women. Doug had had enough of politics in the Church of England. Now he was a simple non-denominational pastor, with a job to do.

Even if he felt any inkling for public politics, which he didn't, a divisive line would be drawn from which there could be no going back. Leave well alone, thank you but no thank you.

The 'phone rang again. Surely not His Worshipfulness so soon? It was the hospital. Thelma had been admitted and had given his name as a contact. Could he come as soon as possible.

Chapter Twelve

He rushed down a corridor searching for the obstetrics unit. He pulled out a piece of paper with the room number he had been given, almost dropping the bunch of flowers in his haste.

There it was, on the left. He knocked. No reply. He entered to see four beds. Thelma was in a bed to the right by a window. She was awake, looking pale and worn. She gave a lame wave. Doug wore his clerical collar, a rare occurrence these days, but experience had taught him that it opens many hospital doors outside visiting hours.

'How you doing, sweetheart?'

'Not so good. They don't know what's wrong, they say it's emotional and I need to be kept an eye on.' Her voice was weary.

'Brought you these to cheer you up, I know they're your favourite.' He laid the large bunch of sunflowers gently in her hands.

She sniffed them with a weak smile. 'Yeah, remind me of the sun. Wally used to, Wally used to, get them for me.' She burst into tears.

Doug pulled the curtain round to allow some privacy, then put his arm round her shoulders. She clung to him.

'They keep telling me to pull myself together Doug, or I'll make my baby poorly. I'm doing my best but I can't seem to get it together.'

'You will darling, you will. You've just got to give yourself time. Is there anything, anything I can help with?'

She shook her head. 'Don't think so. Unless you can get me out of here.'

'OK, I'll see if I can have a word with a doctor and find out what's going on. I'll come back in a few minutes. Alright?'

She nodded. Doug went into the corridor to the reception desk. Eventually a nurse appeared and he asked if it was possible to see a doctor. She went off down the corridor, returning with a lady bearing a stethoscope. Doug explained who he was and that Thelma had no relatives.

He was told Thelma had been found collapsed near her flat by another resident, who called an ambulance. The medical assessment was depression and there were concerns about how this might affect her baby. A scan had shown that the baby was undersized. She needed rest in a suitable environment.

Doug made a decision. He asked if Thelma could be discharged into his care. The doctor replied that would be in her best interest as she should not live alone. Physically she could be discharged straight away and the paperwork would be ready in a few minutes.

Doug told Thelma and she bucked up immediately, slowly

swinging her legs onto the floor.

'Hey, not so fast madam. Take it easy. I'll wait in the corridor while you get dressed.'

Within ten minutes they were walking arm in arm down the corridor towards the exit.

When he had helped her into the car, he said he needed to make a 'phone call and would be as quick as he could.

He walked a short distance, pulling his mobile from a pocket, deep in thought. Better think this through, have a plan. He rang Sally.

She considered what he told her for a moment, then said that she would move into the cottage after work. It would be more company for Thelma and support for him.

Sounds a good idea he thought as he returned to the car. Sally made all the right decisions, saw things in perspective and made good choices. That was one of the reasons he loved her, one of many. She was always there, totally reliable, fully trustworthy. Not unlike Mary in so many respects. He was moving forward in his new era; so different from the downhearted, dispirited man who had entered retirement. Lost, now found. Facing problems he had never experienced before, could never have even dreamed of, but found himself. His true self.

Sally had made up a bed in the spare bedroom and helped Thelma to settle in. Doug had taken her to her flat on the way from the hospital and collected the few belongings she asked for whilst she waited in the car.

It was four days after her discharge and she was on the mend, getting stronger by the day. She was brighter and more positive, saying she would go for a short walk to get some fresh air.

Doug watched her go through the kitchen window.

'She's going to make it.'

Sally joined him, linking his arm. 'Yes, she will. I love you.'

He kissed her. "That's good cos I love you too.'

He looked at the kitchen clock. 'Hey, time to get going. Don't want you getting the sack, we've got a wedding to pay for! And the builder's coming at ten.'

'Oh yes, the garage. Four days you said. We can bring the Pilot over from my place on Saturday, yeah?'

'Hopefully.'

She collected her coat and handbag. Pulling on his coat, Doug collected the car keys from the hall table. Thelma already knew their daily routine and had her own front door key.

When he returned, Thelma was sitting at the kitchen table drinking tea.

'Pot's still hot.' She indicated the teapot on the table.

He reached for a mug and sat down opposite her.

'The builder will be here soon to build a garage for the Pilot.'

Her eyes glazed over. 'Do you remember the good times we had in that car?'

He did indeed. Soon after they met he had taken them for a drive in her. He had asked where they wanted to go for lunch and McDonald's was the unanimous reply. He had never driven through a McDonald's Drive Thru and quite enjoyed the experience. He had driven into the country and they sat in a peaceful lane, munching double cheeseburgers and fries, drinking cans of coke. Ruby was ecstatic as she was constantly fed pieces of cheeseburger.

Doug had looked through the windscreen as he chewed.

How could he help these kids - well a few quid would help for sure but that would only be temporary. His thoughts had been abruptly interrupted by a scream from the back seat.

'You little thieving bastard! You're at it again.'

Wally was about to open a packet of chocolate biscuits which Thelma grabbed viciously.

'I never. I paid for em.'

'Liar!'

She had shouted at Doug that they had been to the supermarket the previous evening to buy necessities with the little money they had. That did not include luxury items.

She had turned her anger to Wally who hunched over like a naughty child.

'You lyin little prick. You're gonna end up in the nick if our probo hears about this.'

She had hit him on the arm, glaring ferociously.

'What else you got?'

'Nuffin.'

'Liar!'

Doug hadn't known what to say. Silence is golden. He guessed anything he might say would be inappropriate and probably pour oil on already troubled water.

Ruby had come to the rescue. She snuggled up to them both, first resting her head on Wally's lap and then Thelma's, growling softly.

'Doug, you tell him. Tell him what prison's like.'

He had not divulged anything about his background to them, and wondered why Thelma assumed he had been to prison. He had visited a prison once when one of his congregation was on remand for alleged fraud and the experience was certainly not pleasant.

'Not somewhere you want to go, Wally. You'd hate being locked up, mate,' he had said lamely.

Thelma had snorted 'It bloody ain't, locked up all the time. But that's where you're going to end up.'

If only they'd known how horribly profound that prediction was. Not for petty shoplifting but an armed robbery he hadn't committed.

An uneasy silence had descended in the Pilot. Ruby had licked Wally's face until he smiled. Thelma had smiled when she licked her and Doug had smiled into the rear view mirror. Suddenly they were all laughing, much to Doug's relief.

Then they had gone fishing in the river near their caravan. Wally had jumped at Thelma's suggestion, beaming all over his face like a child being reprieved from the naughty step, with whoops of joy when he thought he had a catch.

Doug quickly changed the subject. 'How's Serena doing?'

'She's gone all religious, wears a headscarf. Like that bloke of hers but he doesn't have to wear one.'

Doug smiled as he tried to imagine Ashar in a headscarf. He asked what she thought about Serena's conversion to Islam, to which she shrugged.

'Whatever turns you on.'

'That's a bit noncommittal.'

She said she didn't know much about Islam, only what she had heard. Good and bad in every religion, live and let live was her opinion. Doug replied that is true but she must surely have thoughts on Serena and her sudden conversion.

'She's up to something. Not sure if she's really sincere or just doing it for him. She reckons she's got no chance of getting the kid back so is playing a long game, hoping he can pull it off.'

A long game. A very risky game. He supposed that any game is worth a try when there is nothing to lose. He shrugged, not wanting to press Thelma any further.

There was a knock at the front door.

When he opened it he saw the builder and his mate, with a lorry laden with materials in the driveway. He had had the forethought to park his car on the lane. The day was beginning to look brighter.

As he got in the car to collect Sally, he surveyed the day's construction. He had been in and out all day, keeping an eye on the operation and making mugs of tea. He was pleased, the foundation had been laid and he could see how the garage was going to look. He was thankful the weather forecast for the next few days was cold but dry.

They all had tea together, he and Thelma had made a lasagne, aided by Ruby who ate titbits and gave her approval with wags of her tail. Thelma went into the lounge to watch television. They retired to the clickie room to finalise wedding plans before going to the centre. Thelma wanted to go with them. They had brought an extra office chair from Sally's bungalow, much to Ruby's delight.

When Doug had shut the door and was surveying the appropriate list, Sally suddenly laughed.

'Sorry but Peter mentioned today that you might be going into politics.'

'Duff information! Don't know where he heard that, but definitely not true.'

'He hears all sorts of things, knows what's going on at a local level as well as national.'

'Yeah well, having a future wife with an MP for a boss is quite enough politics thank you.'

He looked up, glancing at the door as he lowered his voice.

'Thelma wants to go back to work next week. Doesn't want another sick note. I think it's a good idea, do you?'

'Yes, as long as she stays here.'

'That's already agreed. She can't face the flat at the moment. I can run her, no problem. Just have to know what shifts she'll be working.'

'If they clash with the centre no problem, I can run her.'

'That reminds me, we need to look for a car for you.'

'A sporty little number please, convertible.'

Doug stiffened, thinking of Tracey's MG Midget. She saw his expression.

'Only joking. Sorry.'

He smiled. 'It's OK.' Then as he looked at his watch, 'Hey, time to go.'

Doug and Ruby had returned from taking Sally and Thelma to work and he was having a mug of tea at the kitchen table with that week's *Chronicle* in front of him. He was looking down the *Cars for sale* column of the classified section.

One stood out. Ford Fiesta hatchback, 2016 model, white with charcoal interior, one owner, low mileage, good condition. The price seemed reasonable. He picked up his mobile and dialled the number. A man answered. They arranged a viewing that afternoon. He wrote down the name and address and looked at the clock. Plenty of time.

The garage was coming along nicely. He took out two mugs of tea and surveyed progress. On schedule and a neat job, blended in well with the cottage. And on budget. Not a concrete monstrosity which would stand out like a sore thumb but weathered stones.

A quick lunch and they were on their way. The address was on the other side of the village, on the Maidenbury road. He drove onto the estate of neat three bedroomed properties and looked at numbers. There it is, number thirty-two, on the left. The car was in the driveway.

The doorbell was answered by a man in his early fifties with sharp features and greying hair. They shook hands and Doug looked round the car. Just what he wanted. They went for a test drive, then returned to look at the paperwork which seemed in order. Had just been MOT'd and taxed for eight months. The man had a trustworthy manner, not pushy and willing to answer Doug's questions.

Sally had said she didn't need to see a car, if he thought it OK, go for it. This one seemed perfect. They haggled briefly over the price, agreeing in the middle of the asking price and Doug's offer. The owner said he didn't need a deposit, Doug seemed a man of his word. Collection was arranged for six that evening, he wanted to surprise Sally after picking her up from work.

Doug had been to his bank the previous day and withdrawn enough cash to buy a car in his price bracket. As Doug and Ruby, who had sniffed all round and given her approval by jumping on the passenger seat before the test drive, were walking to their car the man called out.

'I think I know you. Doug. Doug Spencer, local hero. Am I right?'

'Don't know about local hero! But that's my name.'

'Thought so. I'm Robin Johnson, the producer of the local radio program, *Your Space*. You might have heard of it?'

He had and had heard people talking about it.

'Would you be interested in being interviewed by June Towers, our presenter. I'd like listeners to hear about you and your accomplishments in Maidenbury. Can I get her to ring you?'

Doug thought for a few seconds. Not his style, blowing his own trumpet. But on the other hand being able to tell about the centre and food bank seemed a good idea.

'OK, why not.'

Robin said he had his number and June would be in touch soon.

Doug popped home to ring his insurance company for a cover note on the Fiesta. He looked impatiently at the clock in the clickie room as he did so. Why does time go so slowly when you don't want it to? Thelma was working until late so was going direct to the centre. Click, click, click. Ruby preferred the almost inaudible click of the clock to those heavy clicks Dad does on his desk thing. At last it was time.

He collected Sally and as they drove she looked round the area in confusion.

'Where we going, this isn't the way home?'

'Surprise surprise. Wait and see.'

She leaned forward to peer through the windscreen as she

tried to work out where they were. Doug turned into the road and pulled up outside number thirty-two.

She examined his face as he stared impassively out of the windscreen.

'Well?'

'Well what.'

'Oh come on,' she paused as light dawned.

'You haven't bought that, have you?' She stared at the shining Fiesta.

'Might have. Want to have a look?'

She was out of the car in a second.

'Oh Doug, I love her!' she exclaimed as she looked at the car from every angle.

Doug rang the doorbell and Robin appeared. They stood watching as Sally got in the driving seat. Robin went over and shook her hand.

'Reckon she looks right at home, don't you Doug!'

Laughing they went indoors to complete the deal. When they came out, Sally was still sitting in the same place, examining the interior.

'She's yours. Who's driving her home?' Robin asked.

'Me of course. I do know something about cars. Oh thank you, Doug.' She got out and gave him a kiss, chatted briefly with Robin and thanked him, then excitedly took the keys from Doug's open hand.

They both waited for kangaroo jumps as she pulled away. None, went smooth as a whistle.

The garage was finished and the opening ceremony was a

combination of collecting the Pilot and deciding whose car goes where. Carefully Doug edged her into her new home and stood with Sally and Ruby as he pulled down the overhead door. It was decided that Doug would park his car in front of the garage and Sally's would go in the driveway where Doug used to park.

He mused on the time the mobile catering trailer had been parked there, before moving it to the centre of Maidenbury. Bob Planter had taken him to a garage that sold such vehicles and he had bought a well-used but serviceable one. When it was delivered he had parked it in the cottage driveway. He had given it several trials producing hot stew, tea, coffee and other beverages.

The estate already had a towbar fitted, and he had practised driving up and down the road, turning corners though three point turns needed extra attention. Ruby was very puzzled when the trailer arrived, sniffing round and round this strange object taking up the driveway where Dad used to park his car. She soon got used to seeing the estate parked outside on the road, loved scampering up and down inside the trailer whilst Dad stirred pans. Though she was not sure about that thing making dark brown smelly stuff, it had kept hissing at her.

Then it became the focus of attention in Maidenbury, serving the hungry, before he found the centre. Happy times. He remembered the opening night affectionately. The trailer was in place on the appointed council land. Everything was ready. Inside the trailer, with trembling, sweaty hands Doug had unbolted and swung up the serving door, secured the side supporting telescopic rods. He could see people hanging around, others streaming his way.

His mother had loved The Magic Roundabout so had re-named him Dougal instead of the baptized Douglas. He was a fan of *Father Ted* but hoped he wasn't anything like Father Dougal. Not being high church, he preferred Doug as in Rev Doug. He had waved at the sky calling 'Hey ma, if you're listening it's Father Dougal here. Top of the world ma, top of the world!'

He was brought back to present reality by Sally's voice.

'The phone's ringing.'

He dashed into the clickie room and grabbed the receiver as he sat down. He froze.

Chapter Thirteen

He replaced the receiver slowly, sat staring into space for a long time. Sally entered. She looked at him with a worried expression.

'What's up?'

He swung slowly in her direction.

'Tracey's got breast cancer.'

She gasped, cradling his head silently in her arms.

After a while he leant back, deep in thought. He watched her sit in her chair, glimpsed Ruby enter then leave, knowing something bad was happening and wanting to leave them alone. It all seemed to be a dream. Nightmare in a dreamlike state.

He tried to pull himself together.

'She's having a double mastectomy and chemo. Her mother died of breast cancer.'

'Poor Tracey. I don't know that to say.'

He shrugged. 'What is there to say.'

'When are you going to see her?'

'I'm not. She doesn't want to see me, just wanted me to know,' adding 'well not at the moment anyway. Maybe later?'

Going to the centre diverted his mind. It was in full swing. Sally was helping clear away, Thelma getting ready with the choir. He went into the chapel.

Normality in the abnormal. He closed the door and sat down at the back. The sudden silence was comforting at first, then challenging. He had wanted the comfort of normality but needed time to think, get his head together. Pray. He closed his eyes. His visit to Tracey's house to talk about her betrayal flooded uncomfortably into his mind.

'Well, where do we go from here? I don't understand, well I do, work. Getting a story. That's all that matters to people like you, I guess.'

She had looked uncomfortably out of the window. People like you, ouch.

'Yes, I do owe you an explanation. I'm sorry things worked out the way they did, and I'm sorry you felt hurt. It wasn't like that, or rather it isn't what you think.'

'Well it certainly looks like you used me, deliberately got to know me to get a story. To sell your rag and make a name for yourself. Pretty cheap if you ask me.'

She had looked at the floor. He's right, it was a cheap shot. It did start like that, before she got to know him. But then something changed, he became a person, not a news item.

'OK, cards on the table, Doug. I did see a story, a follow-up to the local vicar who got thrown out.' She referred to a story she had written before they first met, a local vicar who had an affair with his secretary.

He had interrupted.

'Ah, you thought I might have some useful secrets, poke around in my closet and see what falls out. Nice one.'

No, not nice. Pretty despicable in fact. How could she know she would get to like him, have feelings. Oh this is hopeless, how could she even begin to explain. Better not to try, only apologise and hope the sore would heal, given time. There would be no quick fix, she knew that.

He had let his emotions pour out, leaving her in no doubt that she had hurt him, deeply. He had trusted her, allowed their friendship to develop under false pretences. How could he trust her again?

More silence. She had made coffee, glad of the break. As she handed him a mug she patted Ruby. She could not remember feeling so down.

As he sipped, a thought had occurred to him.

'How did you know I was a vicar, I never told you.'

She had wondered when he would raise that point. Be honest, tell the truth, no more deception. He was worth more.

'I looked you up on the internet. I asked for your name in the café that first time we met, and well, that was it.'

So that was it. The explanation had not made him feel any better. He had been available, another piece in her complex jigsaw. If the pieces fit, fine. If not make them, cut corners, do whatever is necessary to juggle for a story. Not his world, not the reality he had experienced. He sighed. Was his world so black and white, so concerned with truth and forgiveness and hope that he had missed the point? What was the point?

'Your world is not my world.'

As he spoke the words he thought how pathetic they sounded. Judgemental, pious, holier than thou.

'No it isn't. But because our worlds have collided doesn't mean we can't learn. If we want to".

Did he want to? What the hell DID he want? To his surprise he had crossed the space between them and gently kissed her lips. She had responded, hugged him, pulled him closer with passion.

He shook his head, wanted to forget. It hadn't worked out. Nobody's fault, just fate. Fate! Often described as the development of events outside a person's control, regarded as predetermined by a supernatural power. Bollocks!

He looked at the simple wooden Cross on the table at the front, covered in a plain white cloth. Predestination does not include free will. If everything is already decided, then those predestined to be winners would automatically win and the rest lose. Not only does that seem grossly unfair but discounts free will, which in Doug's opinion is the crux of the argument. We are not robots but are given the choice to make our own decisions in life, good or bad.

He had spent a lot of time since his retirement on contemplating the nature of God. He must write his thoughts down, knock them into shape. For what? He didn't do sermons any more. Would anyone be interested? Possibly, possibly not. So what is the point? God is Love, end of. Tell that to a suffering world. Tell that to Tracey… is that why she rang him, to ask for prayer even though she wasn't sure that she actually believes?

He said a prayer for her and felt more peaceful, then got up and returned to the main room just in time to hear Thelma singing. Hymns from the heart. Oh God, are you listening?

The next morning Doug was running Thelma to work, she was on a twelve to seven shift. He had told her about Tracey the previous evening. She knew her quite well, Tracey and Doug had visited her and Wally at the caravan. Tracey had asked to record an interview there about their life in care together and had written a sympathetic article in the Chronicle. They had also helped together now and again at the centre.

'I've been thinking. I like Tracey. Do you think I could visit her?'

He reflected on her offer. Would she want visitors? She didn't want to see him, not yet at least. But she had contacted him. It might take Thelma's mind off her own problems. Or it could be a disaster.

'Tell you what, why don't you ring her this evening before we go to the centre. Sally's taking you home so you can talk to her and then ring.'

Seems a good idea. And keep Sally in the loop. He realised he was walking on eggshells, he did not want to neglect Tracey but didn't want to upset Sally. Was Sally jealous or was he being paranoid? He couldn't imagine for one moment she would be jealous, that was ridiculous. She understood they were just good friends. Now. OK, maybe she had a feeling that Tracey would have liked more than just friendship, but he was marrying her.

'OK, I'll do that,' she said as she got out of the car and went into the supermarket.

'Am I being super sensitive?' he asked as Ruby jumped into the passenger seat.

At the centre later, Thelma said she had rung Tracey who would like a visit. She was still at home and Sally had offered to run her. He looked at Sally who was talking with a couple of newcomers. I love you sweetheart, I really love you. Why did I ever doubt. She noticed his stare and smiled back. As she drifted past him she whispered 'Tell you later' and kissed his cheek.

An idea occurred to him. Why didn't he take Thelma to visit Tracey and see what sort of a reception he got? If not good, he could wait in the car. He could take Ruby, that would break any ice.

When they arrived home he discussed the idea with Sally and Thelma. They thought it good as long as Thelma checked with Tracey first. They explained the visit was planned for the following afternoon, after Sally finished work. Thelma was on a morning shift.

Doug looked pointedly at the lounge 'phone. Thelma didn't twig at first so he made a suggestion.

'Why don't you ring now, she doesn't go to bed til late.'

Oops, was that insensitive? How did he know information like that? He glanced at Sally who pretended she had not heard the last part.

'Yeah, why not,' Thelma agreed.

I'll put the kettle on,' said Doug.

Arrangements made, they retired to bed. As he pulled back his side of the duvet, he glanced at Sally who was already in bed. He wondered if he was in for a round of uncomfortable questions. He needn't have worried. She snuggled up to him as soon as he got into bed and lay with her head on his chest. She looked at him impishly.

'Long day. Let's get some sleep. In a minute though!' She switched off the bedside lamp, then drew him closer.

At six o'clock the following evening they set off. Doug was nervous, wondering if he was doing the right thing. Tracey hadn't wanted to see him, not yet anyway. What's the worst that can happen? If he got a frozen look, he could mumble that he was just giving Thelma a lift and would wait in the car. She might invite him in, she might warm on seeing Ruby. He would soon find out.

He did not understand that Tracey desperately wanted to see him but was too proud to admit it. When she answered the doorbell her face lit up. She made a fuss of Ruby.

She led them into the lounge. She told Thelma how sorry she was to hear about Wally, giving her a hug. Thelma replied that she was sorry to hear about her illness. Tracey broke the awkward silence by asking if they would like a drink, exiting to the kitchen when she had their request for tea.

'I know what you'd like, young lady,' as she stroked Ruby, 'follow me.' They disappeared.

Doug looked round the neatly furnished room, memories flooding back.

'Nice place,' Thelma whispered. 'Very posh.'

Tracey returned with mugs of tea.

'Mugs today, no china,' she smiled as she handed them each

a mug, returning to the kitchen for hers. Ruby lay beside her chair. Did she sense something, could she smell cancer? Doug had seen a report of recent studies that Labrador Retrievers excel at all types of detection work because of their noses and apparently are able to smell cancers.

They peered at each other over the rim of their mugs.

'Biscuit?' She offered a tin she had brought from the kitchen. Nods and thanks.

More silence.

Thelma broke the ice, bless her. 'Lovely place, Tracey.'

Tracey was animated. 'Thank you. I like it,' adding, 'been here a while now.'

Doug felt he needed to say something, get the conversation going.

'What's the plan Tracey, what does your doctor say?'

She looked at him, then the floor.

'Oh well, the surgeon wants to operate next week. The oncologist says to start chemo soon afterwards. That's about all I know for now.'

She had private health care and her doctor had referred her immediately when he examined the two lumps in her left breast. Good job she had noticed them before it went too far. The prognosis was actually quite encouraging. Just have to get through the treatment.

Doug asked if there was anything he could do. She smiled. 'Pray.'

'Of course. Already on it.'

They looked at each other. Thelma came to the rescue again.

'Life's a bitch ain't it. Always some bastard thing hiding round the corner.'

'I couldn't have put it better myself Thelma! Still, things always work out in the end. One way or another.'

Doug felt she was referring to his loss of Mary and finding a new relationship. At least he thought that was what she was implying. She didn't seem bitter, more 'let's face the music together' attitude. The Fortunes' hit *You've Got Your Troubles* surfaced as he struggled for words. *I see that worried look upon your face You've got your troubles, I've got mine.* He and Thelma were sitting on the very sofa where he had first kissed Tracey. He was filled with nostalgia as he pictured her curled up, trying to cope with her diagnosis and future. Alone.

They stayed a short while longer, chatted about this and that. When they were leaving, he held her hands.

'It'll be alright. Here if need me.'

She forced a smile. The last thing he saw as they drove away was her lonely figure closing the front door.

Chapter Fourteen

Doug felt confused as he replaced the receiver in the clickie room. He stared at the wall, his chair swung restlessly; side to side, side to side, making Ruby feel dizzy until she went back to sleep. She had slept through his long telephone conversation.

June Towers had arranged to ring him today and his interview for *Your Space* had just been recorded for airing next Tuesday.

He had forgotten all about it, was taken by surprise when she rang and more importantly by her questions. They had agreed a rough framework and it had started well. She had introduced him to her listeners in a friendly tone, her opening questions were straight-forward and easy to answer, letting him describe how the centre came about and its success.

Then came the grilling. Mentally he kicked himself for being so naïve and unprepared. True, he had a lot on his mind but even so, he had walked right into it. Too late, it would go out on Tuesday. Maybe the listener ratings would be low that day?

He had come to the part about the need in the town, with growing numbers of hungry people being fed. And that a food bank had recently opened. Lulled into a false sense of security with everything going to plan, her voice had suddenly changed.

'Rev Doug as you like to be called, you are presumably a Christian. There are a lot of Muslims and other minority religions moving into the town. You are accused by some of provoking and stoking a religious war. What is your answer, Rev Doug?'

His mind had raced ten to the dozen. His chair creaked to the point where he thought it would collapse. He knew he had to say something, anything vaguely plausible. Quickly.

'Well, eh, it is true that there are newcomers and, eh, that will inevitably cause tension. Until people get to know each other. Then, eh, everything usually calms down. It has happened in other towns and cities, people learn to live together. And help each other. For example at the centre...'

She had interrupted to vigorously pursue her question.

'Yes, but you stand accused of inciting a religious war. The Racial and Religious Hatred Act 2006 has extended the offence of incitement to racial hatred set out in the Public Order Act 1986 to make it also an offence to stir up hatred against persons on religious grounds. What do you say to that, Rev Doug?'

She had clearly researched this subject.

'Eh, stand accused. By whom?'

'Obviously I can't reveal my sources, but good people in this town.'

She badgered and badgered but realising he was not going

to answer, had terminated the interview.

He needed to talk with Sally. She told him to go straight over.

She was standing at her office doorway, waved as he approached. She welcomed him with open arms, gently pulled him inside.

He hugged her tightly. 'Gosh, I need you!'

She murmured softly, 'Good, I'm here.'

He sat down and she made coffee. He had given her the gist when he rang, but he was relieved to relate the interview in full. When he had unloaded she sat down.

'Sounds nasty and premeditated. What a cheek!'

'I'd put it a bit stronger than that. But hey ho, I walked right into it.'

'You didn't know her intention. How could you.' She squeezed his hand as she handed him a coffee. 'Relax, you're safe now.'

'Who was she talking about? Has someone got it in for me?'

'No darling. Oh there may be one or two discontents, there always are. People can get jealous over the stupidest things. Usually people who don't like themselves so they don't like other people.' She took his hand soothingly. 'Don't worry about it. People aren't all stupid, they can usually see things for what they are, work it out for themselves.'

He nodded, feeling better. He drained the cup and leaned back. Sally was right. People would work out the truth. Hopefully see the interviewer had a hidden agenda. That she was stirring up racial problems for her own dubious ends.

The 'phone rang and he pushed his lists aside as he reached for the receiver. The radio interview had gone out a couple of hours before. He didn't listen.

'Hi Doug, it's Tracey.'

He sat bolt upright. 'Are you OK?'

'Yes. Going in tomorrow, op on Friday.'

'OK. I'm thinking of you, you know that.'

'Yes, thanks. Look, I listened to your radio interview. Load of shit.'

'You could say that!'

'I thought you might be worrying about who said what. So I've made some discrete enquiries. Journalistic ones. There was only one source. Serena Talbot.'

'Oh, I see. Well I don't actually.'

'She wants to muddy the water apparently. Cause unrest to make her case to children's services look better. If her partner looks to be the victim of religious discrimination, the authorities might get scared and back off. Be more tolerant with his custody application. Make any sense?'

'Yes, it does. In a perverse sort of way, it does.'

'Well be careful. I don't know how deep you are in this but it sounds complicated. See you.'

'Bye Tracey, and thanks. You've been very helpful. Let me know how the op goes. Good luck.'

'You mean *God bless* don't you! Keep those prayers going.'

She rang off.

Well well. Serena, you little monkey. He closed his eyes for Tracey.

Doug waved as Sally reversed out of the driveway on her way to work. He went in and placed the breakfast dishes in the sink to soak. Thelma was on an afternoon shift and having a lie in. He looked at Ruby who was licking her bowl. All gone.

As he made coffee, he mentally went through his list for the day. Apart from checking his wedding list, surprisingly it seemed fairly clear.

He took his mug into the clickie room and settled at his desk. He rang Jim and Angela. Beth was out but he hoped to catch her before going to the centre. Thelma needed to get to work but that would fit in. She would walk to the centre when she finished work.

He pulled over the wedding list and ticked off the arrangements he had just made with Jim and Angela. So far so good. Beth just needed to be updated but Angela was in the loop so if he kept missing Beth, Angela could fill her in on the wedding details.

He heard Thelma come downstairs and go into the kitchen. He found her in her flannelette pyjamas and holey dressing-gown, filling the kettle as she yawned. She asked if he wanted a drink to which he replied that he'd just had one. She got out cereal, milk and a bowl and spoon and sat at the table. She sipped coffee from her mug with a picture of Ruby on the front, a gift from Sally. She gave Ruby a few corn flakes which were gone in two seconds.

Doug sat down opposite. He wanted to talk about Serena but was not sure this was the time. Anyway, she probably hadn't seen her since she moved in with them.

'Sleep well?'

She shrugged. 'Sort of,' as she chewed. 'Had a strange dream. Me and Wally when we first met you. At the caravan, remember?'

'Oh yes. How could I forget!'

'He wasn't a thief you know, he, we just needed a little bit extra sometimes, like a packet of biscuits or some crisps. That ain't a crime is it? Wally done it, I done it.'

Not exactly a major crime, an annoyance to the shopkeeper which caused the authorities to put them on probation. To help them when reports showed they were struggling to fit into society. Round pegs in square holes. Two kids from the care system. They had responded though, tried to fit in. In fact they were fitting in nicely when they moved to Maidenbury. Too well in fact. Wally had gone to assist a work colleague and…

'When can I bury him?'

The question took Doug by surprise. Sally was going to talk to her about that, prepare the way for him to talk about the funeral arrangements.

'Well, we need to talk about that, sweetheart. There's no reason why we can't go ahead now the coroner has given permission. You tell me when and we'll go through the details together.'

She stared at him. Given permission. That's rich, given her permission to bury her Wally. About bloody time!

'I don't want him putting in no hole to rot. I couldn't stand that.'

He touched her hand.

'I know. He can be cremated?'

She leaned forward intently, fear in her voice.

'He won't burn in hell will he, Doug?'

He wanted to explain the result of his long meditation on that subject. Since his retirement he had examined his beliefs in a former life, and had found them sadly lacking. Ask a vicar what happens after death and the answer will vary depending on their churchmanship.

Doug had read and re-read Scripture, looked at many religious beliefs, reflected on the nature of God as he understood it. His conclusion was that God is love and does not wish any soul to burn for all eternity. He had pondered long and hard on the text in John's Gospel chapter fourteen, verse two: *In my Father's house are many rooms. If it were not so, would I have told you that I go to prepare a place for you?*

He had come to accept that souls who have not accepted Jesus and done evil, some profound evil, after death go to a room where Jesus teaches them. The very Jesus they had rejected, persecuted. Burning in hell was to his recent thinking a concept thought up by man to exact revenge; a rod by which congregations are kept in line, relieved of their money and forced to attend church, in many cases against their will. In love.

'No sweetheart, he won't. I can't see any way that will happen.'

A burden seemed to lift. She relaxed.

'You know I listen to you Doug, believe what you say.'

He was humbled, challenged. What gave him the right to impose his thinking on Thelma, or anyone? But if he was asked a question, should he lie? To maintain the status quo with deliberate dishonesty.

'I'm not saying I'm right, just that's how I see it.'

She finished the corn flakes, drained her mug and got up.

'I get that. The funeral, we'll do it next Monday, I've got a day off. Is that OK with you?'

He nodded. As far as he could remember he was free all day. He would look in his diary. If he wasn't free, he would make himself free.

As Thelma got dressed in her bedroom he went into the clickie room with Ruby to prepare a draft order of service. He thought he knew what Wally and Thelma would want. Thelma would certainly give her opinion.

Monday morning, eleven o'clock. Dry but cloudy, looked like it might rain. The cottage was quiet. Upstairs, Thelma and Sally were getting ready. Black clothes were banned, Thelma wanted bright clothes and smiling faces.

Doug gathered together his notes, approved by Thelma. She wanted the service to be a short celebration of Wally's life, he wouldn't have wanted any frills. The details of the service had been advertised at the centre for the past couple of days. Thelma did not want anyone other than friends from the centre to attend, plus Joan her boss at the supermarket, Bob Planter and Pastor Jim. The service was set for noon. The funeral director had said the hearse would arrive at eleven forty-five.

When they arrived at eleven-thirty the centre was filling up. The place fell silent as Thelma entered and walked to the chapel with Doug and Sally. People were dressed in the brightest clothes they possessed. Doug wore a Hawaiian shirt over jeans, Sally a flowery dress. Thelma wore a floral print long sleeve dress borrowed from Sally. Ruby had a piece of bright yellow material tucked into her collar.

People moved into the chapel until there was standing room only. There was no pushing or shoving, everyone was very respectful. The remnant stood holding hands in a circle in the main room, heads bowed in silence.

Thelma held Sally's hand tightly. Doug went outside to wait for the hearse. It had started to drizzle. As he positioned himself on the pavement, suddenly he saw a crowd of brightly dressed people moving towards the centre. The thriving second-hand charity shop had been generous in giving away bright clothing over the past couple of days.

They halted as the hearse slowly approached, stopping in front of Doug. He went to the rear and the wicker coffin was carefully lifted out and placed on a bier. Six men suddenly appeared from the centre and placed themselves round the coffin, each taking a handle. They lifted it gently onto their shoulders.

Doug led the way inside with clasped hands as they bore their friend towards the chapel door. The group inside still held hands but moved to form two lanes as the coffin passed.

Thelma sat with Sally on the front row. Ruby lay at Thelma's feet, observing proceedings with an inquisitive expression. She could faintly smell Wally but where was he?

The pallbearers carefully laid the coffin on a large table in front of the altar which was draped in a white linen cloth, leaving a space in front of the altar at Doug's request. They bowed to the coffin and withdrew to chairs reserved at the back. Doug took a large framed photo of Wally from the altar and placed in on the coffin facing the congregation.

Bob Planter had rigged up a big screen on the wall behind the altar, so a grinning Wally looked down on them.

Tracey wanted to publish an article in the Chronicle to go with her *Justice for Wally* campaign and took discrete photos at the back. Thelma had willingly given her permission.

Doug stood in the narrow space, putting his hands on the coffin as he looked at the congregation.

'Dearest Thelma, dear friends. Here we are, a day we never thought would come. Celebrating Wally's short life.' He pointed to the picture on the wall behind him.

'That's our Wally. The guy we all knew and loved. Not perfect, who is, but with Wally what you saw was what you got. Sincerity. Always. He ended up in care and fought with Thelma to get out. He came here, with Thelma and helped so many. Some of you are here today. Wally always said '*Life's a bitch, then you die.*' There were murmurs of appreciation.

'For Wally life could be a bitch. Until he got to know you all and found love and support. Then he died. Killed mercilessly by an unjust, cruel system which eventually consumed him, sucked the life out of him. Because he couldn't fight it any more. Oh he tried, our Wally gave it his all but in the end too many odds were stacked against him.'

He turned to the wall image, outstretching his arms in salute.

'Thank you Wally. For just being you. A good lad and a faithful friend.'

The congregation were on their feet, arms outstretched as the name *Wally* rung round the room.

Doug waited until they were seated, then proceeded with the service. Jim gave the eulogy, starting with Wally meeting Thelma and their running away together. There wasn't a dry eye. He concluded with the 23rd Psalm which many recited by heart and with heart. Doug offered prayers of thanks for his life and a reading chosen by Thelma, ending with the committal.

He gave a blessing and invited people to go forward, Thelma first, to say their personal goodbyes. They gathered round the coffin, hands on Thelma, many weeping. Despondent despair hung in the air.

As they slowly moved away, they touched the coffin, most kissing it.

Doug and Sally put their arms round Thelma and supported her sobbing body between them as they led the mourners into the main room. At the chapel door, Thelma stopped and looked back at the coffin.

'Do I have to leave him? I can't, he'll be so lonely. My Wally, my beautiful boy.' Doug caught her as her knees gave way.

They looked after Thelma as best they could, talking in the cottage when she was not at work and keeping her mind occupied. The funeral had brought reality crashing down; before she had seemed to exist in a sort of Neverland, a place where everything would go away.

They made sure she was not in ear range when they talked about their wedding; played music she enjoyed, watched her favourite television programs with her. They did not mention the baby, waited for her to bring it up in her own time.

Doug attended hospital appointments with her, there were still concerns for her mental health and the effect on the baby.

They were watching the previous evening's *EastEnders* on catch-up one evening before going to the centre, when the storyline must have triggered something.

'I'm going to have the baby adopted,' came out of the blue.

Doug looked at Sally. Was this a cry for help? There had not been a hint of this when they had talked previously, she seemed to be looking forward to the birth.

'Wow, when did you decide that?' Doug asked carefully.

'At the funeral. No point now Wally's not here.'

Her tone of voice indicated there was no discussion to be had, she had made up her mind. Perhaps if they gave her time, waited, she might come round? They had thought about how she might cope, her role as a mother, on several occasions; child care, learning to be a single parent, how a baby would fit into her future plans, now or later.

Slowly Doug said, 'Adoption may seem the answer now but why not wait and see how things pan out?'

She stared at him. 'Nope. I've thought a lot about it, made my mind up. I want you to get in touch with that woman you know please, the one who works at the council.' She returned to the screen adding, 'Joan wants me to be a supervisor, says I'm ready. And I'm going back to live in the flat tomorrow.'

The next morning Doug and Sally had arranged to meet at her office. They couldn't talk at the cottage, though they had wanted to discuss Thelma's news straight away. There wasn't time at the centre and Thelma had gone back to the cottage with them afterwards.

She kissed him as he entered. Coffee was ready.

'Well, what can I say. Surprise surprise.'

'She needs to move on. She's scared Doug. She knows deep down she can do it but she's worried she might fail. We know she won't but… I'm helping her to move back into the flat after work.'

'What about the baby?'

'Only she can make that decision. Anyway, I suppose the adoption process is designed to safeguard all parties.'

'I'm going to see Dawn Adams this morning. Get the ball rolling.'

'It won't happen overnight so Thelma will have plenty of time.' She paused. 'Oh, what's happening with Serena and Ashar? Any progress?'

'Not sure, seems to be moving forward. Slowly. Ashar is doing well with his contact sessions, seems very committed.'

'Good. We'll be married soon. Seems sad we have so much happiness, when others we know don't.'

He hugged her. 'Hey, it hasn't all been sweetness and light for us, darling. There has been a lot of darkness we've had to deal with.'

'I know. Perhaps that is why we appreciate what we have now.' She kissed him until Peter's voice called through his office door 'Sally, can you come in please.'

'See you later,' as he made for the front door.

She blew him a kiss as she reached for her notepad and made for Peter's office.

∝

Dawn looked as frumpy as ever, the ill-fitting dress hung like a tent round her increasingly ample form.

She thanked him for his reports on Ashar's contact sessions. She was unable to provide any further information other than to say that matters were progressing.

Doug told her about Thelma's decision to have her baby adopted. She replied that he would need to contact the fostering and adoption team and gave him a card. There were always parents waiting to adopt.

He stared at the card. So Thelma simply hands over her baby when it is born and that's it. New family, new life. For better or worse. He had no experience of adoption but had met several people who had been adopted. Their experiences were mostly positive, they regarded their adoptive parents as their natural parents.

He wondered if the child would ever look for their mother. Would Thelma want that? What would her life be like at that stage?

As he put the card in his pocket and said goodbye, he pondered the outcome if Wally was still alive.

Chapter Fifteen

The big day arrived on a sunny, crisp morning. Valentine's Day. The centre was packed. Bob Planter had rigged up a large screen so the ceremony could be relayed from the chapel. Every seat there was taken by ten-forty. There was a mixture of invited guests and many who wanted to support their beloved Rev Doug, all waiting with excited expectation.

At ten-fifty Sally arrived in the shining Pilot with white flowers on the bonnet, chauffeured by Ashar who was dressed in an impressive dark grey suit, white shirt and matching tie. He had been given suitable training for the task. He was a good driver but his charge was precious. Tracey accompanied Sally, the back seat adorned in a spotless white silk sheet.

It had been Tracey's request to accompany Sally. Her operation had been successful, a decision was to be made soon whether chemotherapy and/or radiation were needed. She was hopeful the answer would be negative.

Ashar opened the rear door of the Pilot, bowing as they alighted. They went into the centre to cheers and claps. The door was held open with a toothless grin by one of the regulars, who like all the regulars present was dressed in his definition, or availability, of smart. Sally smiled appreciatively as they entered.

She held Tracey's arm as they looked at the assembly. Local dignitaries, her boss, Bob Planter, Dawn Adams; wow, everyone they knew.

The Elvis Presley version of *Can't Help Falling in Love* started playing, courtesy of Bob. Sally wore a light blue two-piece matching jacket and skirt and white silk blouse with fringed trim, Tracey a dark blue dress.

As they processioned down the centre with people on both sides, Thelma was at the chapel door to greet them. They entered the chapel and there at the front stood Doug with Jim, the latter in clerical collar and black suit. Sally smiled to herself as she wondered the last time Jim had worn his ecclesiastical outfit. Actually she preferred his jeans and T-shirt, they were much more him. Doug wore a charcoal grey double-breasted suit, white shirt and grey tie, bought for the occasion.

As they went up the aisle, Angela and her partner Joe, Beth and Doug's three grandchildren stood up on the front row. The congregation rose.

Doug and Jim stood in front of the altar. When they reached Doug, Tracey moved to stand in front of the only available chair, reserved for her.

The couple stood facing each other, hand in hand. Their smiles needed no interpretation.

Jim nodded and the music stopped.

'Dear family and friends, we are gathered here today in the

sight of God to join Sally and Doug in holy matrimony. Sally, please repeat after me:

Doug, I promise to cherish you always, to honour and sustain you, in sickness and in health, in poverty and in wealth, and to be true to you in all things until death alone shall part us.'

Sally repeated the words as she gazed lovingly into Doug's eyes.

'Doug, please repeat after me:

Sally, I promise to cherish you always, to honour and sustain you, in sickness and in health, in poverty and in wealth, and to be true to you in all things until death alone shall part us.'

Doug repeated the words, his eyes and thoughts reflecting that he would always cherish her the way he cherished her at that moment.

'Please exchange rings.'

Angela whispered in Mark's ear and gave him the small white silk pillow she had made to bear the rings. He went to Doug, holding up the pillow, thankful his mum had tied the rings loosely with bows of ribbon as his hands were shaking.

Ruby had been surveying the scene from Angela's feet, resplendent in her bow the colour of Sally's suit, her tail wagging gently. When Mark moved she moved, going to sit beside Dad, causing ripples of laughter.

Doug took Sally's ring and gently placed it on the fourth finger of her left hand.

'My darling, I give you this ring as a symbol of my eternal love.'

Sally took Doug's ring and placed it on his ring finger, repeating the same words.

Jim beamed as he savoured the moment. Then noting the

'Get on with it' glance from Doug, he proclaimed:

'I now pronounce you man and wife. You may kiss the bride.'

They kissed, not a lingering kiss but full of passion.

Jim said a short prayer of blessing and the couple led the way into the main centre, followed first by family and Tracey, then the rest of the congregation. The shouts and applause as they entered were deafening.

During the ceremony tables had appeared, laden with plates of food. Non-alcoholic sparkling wine was served by the centre helpers, out of respect for the majority who were recovering alcoholics. Music played, people ate, drank and danced.

As the plates and cutlery were cleared away for the evening meeting, cries of 'Speech' rang out. That was one item missing from Doug's lists.

Tracey help up her hand, clicking her glass with a fork. Doug and Sally took a deep breath. What was coming?

'Ladies and gentlemen.' She paused as judging by the ensuing laughter some found that phrase highly amusing.

'Ladies and gentlemen.' Muted laughter. 'It is a pleasure to be here today to celebrate the union of a very special couple. We all know and appreciate what Doug has done for this town, is still doing. Now supported by Sally, the future of this community looks bright.' She raised her glass. 'I give you Doug and Sally.'

Glasses were raised; cheers swelled the room, Doug and Sally breathed a sigh of relief. They were thankful for her gracious words. When they looked back, they realised they had not doubted her. Slightly nervous better expressed their feelings.

More speeches followed, from the known and the unknown. The haves and the have nots, contentedly blending together in a brief moment of time. Finally there were shouts of 'Groom,

groom.'

Sally gave him an encouraging smile.

'Friends, family, thank you for coming and making this a day to remember. And thanks to Pastor Jim for helping us to tie the knot.' He raised his glass to Jim who raised his in reply.

'And a special thanks to my darling Sally, for agreeing to be my wife.'

The room erupted. Glasses were raised, kisses blown in her direction.

'Today is the first anniversary of our centre. I raise my glass in salute to each and every one of you. I didn't make this happen, you did. We did it together. And now, clear off because we've got to get ready for tonight's meal! Cheers.' He raised his glass. The room responded.

As people were leaving, Doug made a beeline for Tracey.

'You OK?'

'I suppose.'

'You were brill. Thanks for what you said.'

'What did you expect? I thought we were going to get married but he ran off with another woman? Not my style, Doug.'

There was not a lot to say so he was quiet. She smiled as she introduced a difficult conversation breaker.

'I'd really love to drive the Pilot again. You won't want to leave her outside here all evening. What if I drive her to your place and maybe Ashar would pick me up. Don't worry, I'll be super careful!'

'I know you will. Tell you what, we've got to nip home to get changed. You drive her and we'll follow. Come in for a coffee and I'll drop you at your place on my way back here.

How's that sound?'

'Fine.'

'OK. Just let me say goodbyes and we'll get going. Oh, and I'll tell Ashar what's happening.'

He circulated with Sally, looked at the wedding gifts piled on a table in the corner and acknowledged the well-wishers. They chatted with Angela and Beth and the kids, gave the children a small gift with a larger one for Mark. Angela had said he would appreciate a model of the Pilot and Sally had found one online.

Jim said he had to get off to prepare at his centre and Doug told him he would be in touch soon. As they embraced, Jim whispered, 'Blessings bro, all heaven rejoices.'

The helpers, led by Thelma, were already returning the centre to normality as Doug left with Sally and Tracey.

Doug guided her into the garage and Tracey killed the Pilot engine. She handed him the keys with the comment, 'There you are sir, not a mark!'

Her first drive in the classic flashed into his mind, when they had visited the lockup after their reconciliation following his discovery of her duplicity.

'Ready to go for a spin?' he had asked.

'You bet!'

As they drove, she had delicately inhaled the smell of leather, gazed at the immaculate roof lining and admired the chrome door handles and window winders.

After a few miles she had asked gently if she might have a drive. Doug nodded and pulled over.

She had handled the classic like a pro; changing the column

gears without a sound, constantly listening to the sound of the engine, checking the dashboard instruments as she glanced at them from time to time.

'Heaven Doug, pure heaven!' she had exclaimed as she changed smoothly into second gear, accelerated and moved the lever down into top gear.

Eventually she had pulled up outside the unit doors and turned to him with a disappointed expression.

'I could drive her all day Dougie, such a shame to stop. Do we have to?'

He had looked into her eyes, read the pleasure of a true enthusiast.

His reflections were interrupted, she was talking to him.

'Where's that coffee you mentioned?'

Sally was already inside. They sat in the lounge, three friends enjoying each other's company.

Tracey put down her cup thoughtfully. 'You ought to write a book, Doug'

'You are joking!' he replied, bursting out laughing. 'About what?'

'About your life. How the centre started, what came before. It would be superb.'

'What a good idea, Tracey,' Sally commented enthusiastically.

He was outnumbered. He ruminated back to his early days at the cottage with a shudder. Those were the days my friend, he thought they'd never end. No Mary, no Ruby. A lonely vacuum of despair, a vacuum that was truly filled.

The hours he had sat in the clickie room, trying to fulfil his promise to Mary. To write the memoirs of his ministry. He remembered his efforts all too well which ultimately had culminated in pressing the delete button. No more book.

He looked at Tracey, reflected on his hours in the clickie room, they seemed as clear and as painful as if they were yesterday.

He had made notes, vague plans tossing in his mind like a broken tumble drier. Tossing round and round, doing nothing. He had told himself to make some heat, stop faffing around making excuses. There would be heat, oh yes. Ruffled feathers.

He had told himself humorously that he was becoming a fully paid up member of the creative writers' club. How much truth should go in? Mary had hoped for a positive journey with happy anecdotes, a sort of glorious autobiography.

He didn't see it like that, feeling it should be a journey yes but with warts and all. It would be controversial, open to interpretation which would create the heat. There is heat and heat. Flames when fanned can quickly get out of control. Good, bring it on!

He had concentrated his mind and ideas had started to flow, slowly at first. Then faster and faster, almost overwhelming in their intensity. Surely a clergyperson should be the most likely person to at least claim to have the answers. Perhaps that is the problem.

He looked at Tracey.

'No, don't think so. Thanks for the thought, but no.'

To his surprise Sally jumped in.

'Doug, you need to do this, or at least give it some serious thought.'

'I could help to write it, be a sort of ghost writer,' Tracey added.

He felt he was being dragged down a road he didn't want

to go. He had started his memoirs from a position of despair, putting into words his sense of failure, anger even. About losing Mary; his feelings of having played the game, been a good boy, not rocked a sinking boat. Seeking answers to his own lame questions.

He was a little hesitant about his refusal. Maybe, just maybe, this time he could perhaps tell a story about how life can work out if you try. He had managed to pull himself out of the retirement rut, dealt with bereavement at the same time. Could he possibly help others in a similar situation?

He drained the cup he had been cradling with both hands, coming to a decision.

'OK. Nothing lost in giving it a try. But you do the lists, Tracey!'

'Oh I will, gladly. It's not like I'm starting from scratch, I do know a lot of what went on.'

Doug glanced at Sally to gauge her reaction. Her encouraging smile said it all.

✠

A couple of evenings later, Ashar turned up at the centre. He popped in now and again, got on well with the people and helped clear away after meals. He wanted a word with Doug and they went into the chapel whilst Thelma and the choir were singing.

'There is a court hearing next week about whether I can look after Basma. I think it's going to be OK. The guardian has told me not to worry, Serena has given her consent, all reports seem to be fine. Will you be there?'

'Of course, if you want me. I won't be able to say anything

unless I'm specifically asked. What does your solicitor say?'

'He hasn't mentioned you being a character witness or anything.'

'Well, the only thing I could possibly say to the family court is if asked about your contact with Basma. I've sent written reports anyway.'

'Thank you. I know I shouldn't worry but it's a big thing, caring for my daughter.'

'Of course it is.'

Doug thought about Serena's intention. Let him be granted custody and then move in? All the signs were that he would get custody. But was he strong enough to cope on his own without the mother? He knew this would have been given careful consideration by the authorities. They had observed parenting classes and contact between father and child. Contact sessions had been arranged for this purpose beyond the Saturday contact at the centre.

If Ashar stayed in Manchester permanently, would Serena follow? What would happen if they were caught out? Serena was a no-go area as far as the authorities were concerned. Would this change? Possibly, possibly not. If they could prove a strong relationship with Ashar as the main carer, it was a possibility.

Doug found out later that custody of Basma was granted to Ashar. He lived permanently in Manchester and had returned to his work managing the kebab shop. Basma was with him at his workplace and flat above in the interim and he would arrange appropriate childcare when necessary as she developed, as any parent does.

Ashar and Serena's relationship survived and she went back to Manchester, officially living alone in a flat nearby. The upshot was that Serena was allowed to live with Ashar and their daughter, as long as he respected that he had custody and did not allow harm to come to the child. Serena showed that she accepted the arrangement and was content to live with Ashar and help to look after Basma.

When Doug heard the news he was overjoyed. His initial comment to Sally when he told her was, *There is a God*. Who often moves in very mysterious ways.

Tracey was true to her word, though she was sufficiently computer savvy to put everything on her laptop rather than writing lists. She ghosted a detailed background of Doug's struggle and how the centre was born, including the food bank. She skipped over their relationship and Doug's marriage, focusing on what she considered relevant. She went into detail about Wally, feeling this was part of her campaign *Justice for Wally*.

She met with Doug at regular intervals to discuss progress; got feedback and edited the text. Stage by stage she deleted the notes made on her laptop. The list got shorter. She felt satisfied, her long evenings had been creative. She had returned to work and all tests were clear. Her days had returned to normality, her evenings and weekends filled with typing and retyping the manuscript. On bright weekends she drove the MG with the top down, hair-scarf protecting her from the wind which she always found exhilarating, letting her cares blow away.

This particular evening Doug, Sally and Tracey were sitting in the clickie room going through the final manuscript. Ruby found it rather boring as she lay observing them but understood something important was happening. She enjoyed the treats

Sally kept feeding her, so felt part of the editorial meeting.

'Well, it's finished. Been checked, edited and checked again. Ready to go.'

'That's the point, go where?' Doug asked.

'Always options. I suggest we self-publish and then market it. This would be the cheapest option. I can arrange the self-publishing, and I've got a friend Norma who will help with online marketing. Marketing is essential, otherwise it will just become one of thousands of books on Amazon nobody will ever get to read. Because they don't know it's out there.'

'Yes, I see that,' Sally interjected. 'Make's sense, Doug.'

'Who are we aiming at?' Doug looked confused.

'Well, it's a book for women mainly.' She had an idea. 'Hey, what about the US market? I can see the ladies in the Bible Belt lapping it up! It's just their sort of book.'

'I see where you're going. Love, hope, Christianity,' Sally commented.

'Not forgetting those who have just entered retirement, especially those struggling with bereavement as well,' he added.

'That's who you want to reach, Doug.'

He nodded slowly. 'It's strange. I started writing then deleted it. Now we have the finished article of a complete re-write. How times change.'

'Just shows what a difference having an old pro on board can make!' said Tracey.

They laughed. Doug looked at Tracey.

'Hey, we're all in our prime! But yes, your help has been invaluable, Tracey. Thank you' He grinned at her.

She blushed. 'My pleasure, I've enjoyed it. Ready for the next one.'

'Oh, there won't be a next one. This was quite enough.'

Sally smiled at him. 'Who knows. You've got lots more to say.'

Tracey wondered how the story might have ended if they had stayed together. Their story. She thought of their break-up over his belief that she only got to know him, cultivated their relationship, because she hoped for an inside story on church misconduct, naughty vicars. That was until they got to know each other. And she fell in love.

They had enjoyed each other's company and their love of classic cars. Happy times, like when she took fish and chips to the cottage when he had invited her for dinner during their reconciliation. She had felt his cooking lacked a certain something but didn't want to offend. They had both laughed so much.

And when she was cooking a meal at her house and he had brought her a lovely bunch of flowers. A hug for him, a pat and bowl of food for Ruby and they were sitting in the dining room eating homemade steak pie, mashed potatoes and carrots. Tracey had loved the flowers, put them in a vase on the windowsill.

She had raised her glass and they toasted each other, the medium-bodied, mildly sweet, Riesling going down well.

'To a sincere and creative journalist,' was Doug's toast.

She had smiled as their glasses touched.

Then they had sat on the settee together, sipping from bone china cups. 'Well it isn't really a mug occasion,' Doug had chuckled.

His moment had arrived.

'Tracey, do you know of any soup kitchens in the area?'

That was the beginning of the centre. She had anticipated several possible questions but this had taken her completely by surprise.

He had told her about Thelma and Wally, how they had introduced him to Jim's soup kitchen, well centre for the homeless.

'And you want to get involved in something similar round here?' She had been sceptical.

He had nodded. Not with conviction but as a man searching for answers.

Tracey had been concerned. This man she was liking more and more, growing deeply fond of if she was honest, this good compassionate person was trying to find something in his retirement that he considered lacking in his ministry. She was filled with sadness, she had little idea what was driving him but something clearly was. No, not driving, haunting. By what? His bereavement? No, it was more than that. An emptiness that transcended emotional loss, a void that seemed to dig deep into his very being. Underpinning his daily life, a period which should be coming to terms with the past and seeking new horizons. Moving on.

She had asked, 'Are you certain this is what you want to do, Doug?'

'Yes. I think so.'

You think so? Oh Doug, darling Doug, thinking isn't enough. There is such a long way between thought and action.

She had made a decision.

'Tell you what, I have a friend who works in the council welfare department, Dawn Adams. Why don't I ask her what she knows, she'll be able to tell me what's happening, or not.

OK?'

That was how it all started. And they had ended. Not straight away but a gentle parting. She still did not understand why, there was no definitive point that had manifested itself other than a gradual drifting apart. Perhaps they were just not meant to be. Perhaps she should have tried harder. Perhaps... Doug interrupted her thoughts.

'Have we got a lot more to say, Tracey?'

She smiled and said she had to get home. No Doug, we haven't. You have, you and Sally, but I'm only the editor of your story.

Chapter Sixteen

Doug and Sally were returning from the centre a few evenings later, nearly at the cottage, when his mobile rang. He pulled over and looked at the screen. Jim. Strange, Jim doesn't normally ring at this time.

'Hi Jim, how's things?' The voice on the other end was different from any he had known.

'Doug, just want to warn you. I've heard from some guys at our centre this evening that some evangelical churches in your area are planning a demonstration against you. About your acceptance of Islam, apparently they see you as a threat to their fundamental beliefs.'

Jim did not have further details but told him to be on the lookout.

As he turned into the cottage driveway he looked at Sally.

'Not sure what to make of that. Who's planning what and why? Come on, let's get inside and have a brew.'

They went into the kitchen. He put the kettle on thoughtfully. Sally sat at the table in silence, her mind racing. After several minutes she spoke.

'I think we need to get Peter involved in this. If he isn't aware, he needs to be.'

Doug nodded. If Peter had heard anything he would have mentioned it. So these people, whoever they are, are organizing a demonstration. Fundamentalists. He wanted to laugh. Fundamental Christians and fundamental Muslims. Always at war. Why couldn't he be left in peace to get on with his life, his mission, his resurrection?

He shared his thoughts with Sally over a mug of tea. When having doubt, drink tea! He talked of his understanding about Christianity and Islam. The first need in presenting Islam to people of a Christian background is to understand and acknowledge their fears. Often because of ignorance.

On the face of it, few notice how much Christianity and Islam are alike in basic beliefs. On the five pillars of Islamic belief: the belief in God, angels, the prophets, the sacred books, and the Day of Judgement, there is no basic disagreement. Christians also believe in all of these, although they would define the one God in three persons and take one prophet and one sacred book fewer than in Islam. But all agree on the principles.

Unfortunately, reality is not that simple. That extra book and prophet are most essential to Islam, to say nothing of the absolute unity of God, whereas the five pillars, to the Christian, miss some of the basic issues.

One of the fundamental differences between Islam and Christianity is that while Islam has a basic set of beliefs in common to nearly all who claim to be Muslims, there is hardly anything that is common to all of Christianity. There are important exceptions in all major Christian beliefs and although most Christian denominations are members of the top ten, there are about twenty thousand Christian sects, some of which are more visible in propagation than their number of adherents would suggest. That is why it is necessary from the beginning to find out what the individual believes. One cannot make assumptions.

'Mm, interesting,' she commented. 'I reckon that radio interview you did opened the gate for this demonstration, whatever it is.'

'Yes. Don't know if I told you, but Basma's foster mother is a member of a fundamental Christian church. I wonder if she's been muddying the water?'

'No you didn't mention it, but it makes sense. So what are you going to do?'

'Wait. Wait and see what, if anything, happens. Deal with it then. Right now I suggest we get some sleep.'

'Good idea,' adding with a cheeky smile, 'bed and see what pops up!'

He kissed her as they put their mugs in the sink.

'Hey, I almost forgot to tell you with so much going on. I've accepted an offer on the bungalow. A good offer.'

'Great. So I'm going to bed with a rich woman.'

'Ha, don't know about that. But it will sweeten the pot a little.'

They always said goodnight to Ruby.

'Good night Ruby,' they chimed in unison. She was already asleep, cuddled up in her basket.

Sally knew Peter would be in the office the next morning, so Doug followed the Fiesta in his estate. Peter was glad to see him as they entered his office. Doug filled him in on what he knew.

'Bloody hell, that's all we don't need, a religious war. Why can't they all just support the same team?'

'Yeah, your team! Make them all Arsenal fans.'

'They could do a lot worse.'

As Sally entered with coffee she wondered what they were laughing about. She sat down, sipping expectantly.

Peter said prevention is better than cure. Demonstrations are fully legal in a democracy but not if things get out of hand. He would make enquiries and if he found anything he would let them know, although they were unlikely to hear until it actually happens. So best to wait and see, anyway, with a bit of luck it might never happen. He had regular meetings with Muslim businessmen and nothing had been mentioned.

They talked about Ashar and Serena. In Manchester a young Muslim lady social worker had been allocated to Basma's case who apparently was being tougher on Ashar than the previous incumbent, which was interesting. The consultant social worker was still involved and had reported that everything was on track. His new social worker was taking a strong line and had warned him that he must not let his care of his daughter be compromised by any inappropriate relationship. It was a balancing act; the welfare of the child, supporting her father and guarding any relationship or relationships which could compromise matters for them both.

'Glad I don't have that responsibility!' commented Doug.

'Yes, we'll leave it to the professionals,' was Peter's reply.

The following week Doug and Sally opened the centre as usual. People streamed in and were fed. Thelma led the choir as usual and a comforting normality abided. Until the choir were drowned by shouts from outside.

Doug rushed out to be confronted by a largish vocal group brandishing placards: *This is a Christian country*; *Christ is our Saviour, not just a prophet*; *God NOT Allah*.

They were carrying torches and he could make out some faces in the darkness but none he recognised. They didn't seem to have a leader, though a middle-aged man with a megaphone led the chanting, repeatedly shouting the slogan *Our land, our God*.

Doug watched and waited. Silent defiance might work, the wrong words could incite violence. Should he go back inside and let them burn themselves out? Or would that cause more protest? Would they come back another night, keep coming back?

Suddenly he was aware that Sally and Thelma were by his side. Then a stream of people from the centre joined them until they filled the pavement, possibly out-numbering the protestors.

Thankfully no-one with him spoke, they simply stood in silent protest. A stand-off. Until Thelma stepped forward.

She held up her hand. To his amazement the chanting stopped. Was this what they wanted, to be acknowledged? By a heavily pregnant young woman?

'I know some of you, you shop in the supermarket where I work. You talk about God, well I was just singing His praise when you rudely interrupted. I'm going to sing it for you now.'

She broke into the hymn and as she started the choir joined in:

> *Love one another.*
> *This new commandment*
> *I give unto you*
> *Love one another.*
> *By this shall men know*
> *Ye are my disciples,*
> *If ye have love*
> *One to another.*

When the singing finished there was silence. The protestors looked at one another, then slowly started to disperse. The hymn had clearly touched a nerve. Eventually they stood alone. Doug hugged Thelma and whispered 'Well done you. A hundred speeches couldn't have done what you just did.'

They went back inside and carried on like nothing had happened.

Back at the cottage, Doug and Sally sat with their new ritual, Horlicks in front of the fire. They went over the evening's events. Doug wasn't sure that his approach had been the right one, perhaps he should have taken the bull by the horns and been more assertive? Sally felt they had all acted in the best possible way, letting matters run their course. Anyway, Thelma had saved the day, her approach had been spot on.

Doug sipped the sweet liquid thoughtfully. He was sick

of shadows. Why was everything good always enveloped in shadow? Why were people so divided, divisive? A thousand whys, no answers.

He jumped. Tracey, he must ring Tracey and ask her to write about the evening's events in *The Chronicle*. And on her blog. He wasn't quite sure what a blog is but she did and used it very successfully by all accounts. He made a mental note to contact her first thing in the morning.

Ruby sniffed the sweet smell in the air, savoured the peace which had descended as she observed them from her spot on the carpet. Wouldn't it be nice if humans could see things through a dog's eyes…

$$\propto$$

The next morning he rang Tracey to tell her about the events of the previous evening. She was surprised and commented: 'Don't talk to me about bloody Christianity, there're all religious bigots. Nutcases.'

Difficult to argue, Doug reflected. He thought of the text in Matthew's Gospel chapter seven:

'Do not judge, or you too will be judged. For in the same way you judge others, you will be judged, and with the measure you use, it will be measured to you. Why do you look at the speck of sawdust in your brother's eye and pay no attention to the plank in your own eye?'

'You've got a point there Tracey, you've got a point.'

'OK, leave it with me. I'll write something in the 'paper and on my blog. Give 'em hell. While you're on Doug, what about writing an article every week for *The Chronicle*? I've been thinking about that, you're the man to tell a few home truths.

We could call it the *Wayside Pulpit*.'

Doug thought about it. What harm could it do? Maybe it could be helpful, bring some sanity to a mad society. Oh sure, you aren't going to change the world but, well, perhaps a few weekly well-chosen words might influence our small part of it for the better.

'OK, I'll do it. Give it a whirl anyway.'

'Great. Be in touch.' She rang off.

Doug leaned back in the office chair as it creaked in complaint. Ruby looked up at him. Dad's in thinkie mode again, best to go back to sleep. What should he write about in his first article? Christians and Muslims seemed a good place to start. Or it may be too controversial? Maybe start with something gentle to open, ease his way in. He thought of Jesus easing His way in. Not really, told it like it is. And the people listened as He talked in parables they could relate to.

The 'phone rang.

'Me again. Meant to tell you before, we've got a publisher. Highly recommended. He likes the manuscript and has agreed to publish. It will cost more than self-publishing but I think will be worth it. Oh, and your deadline for the *Wayside Pulpit* is the day after tomorrow. Byee.'

A good job Sally has sold the bungalow, he thought. But they would have managed anyway. The 'phone rang again. Thinking it was Tracey he said, 'Hello, Doug Spencer here, author and sometime journalist.'

'Well that's good to know. Is there no end to your talents?' It was Dawn Adams to tell him that a lovely childless couple had been identified to adopt Thelma's baby. Introductions had been made and Thelma liked them very much.

Doug thanked her and rang off. Thelma had gone very quiet lately on the adoption issue. He and Sally had wondered why. Perhaps she felt guilty.

They were convinced she had made up her mind and would not go back on her decision.

$$\infty$$

The book was published and the essential marketing had begun on several social media platforms. *Phoenix Dawn* by Doug Spencer and Tracey Harrison was hitting newspapers and book bloggers, receiving great reviews.

Sally had just gone to work and Doug was making coffee when the 'phone rang. He went into the clickie room and as he sat at the desk he wondered who was calling at this time of the morning.

'Doug Spencer?'

When he affirmed, a voice said 'Good morning Mr Spencer. My name is Ben Elliott, I'm producer of *Debate UK* which you may have seen on BBC morning television.' He paused for a response.

'Well yes, I have seen it,' he admitted.

'I understand Doug. May I call you Doug?' He continued without a reply. 'Good. Look, I'll come to the point. I have read your book and we would like to interview you on our program. We think our viewers would want to hear about the centre and the work you are doing. Our presenter, Jane Atkinson, would like to do a Zoom meeting with you to go over how the interview will work and the questions she will ask. The interview will take place in our Bristol studio a week on Wednesday. How's that sound?'

It certainly blew away any Monday morning blues he might have felt. It would be good publicity for the book. He was about to give a positive response when the radio interview entered his mind like a storm. This TV interview could really cause problems if it goes wrong. But how can it go wrong, with a Zoom meeting to discuss the questions to be asked and…

'You still there Doug?'

'Yes, I'm here. Just thinking, eh, Ben. What guarantee do I have there won't be extra questions, a trap if you see what I mean.'

'Got you Doug. Understand. Look, you have my word there will be no deviation from the agreed script. What you agree with Jane is what you'll get. We are the BBC, we don't do traps.'

Oh yeah, and I'm a dancing orangutan came into his head as he silently considered the offer.

'I need to discuss this with my co-author Tracey Harrison before I can give you an answer. But yes, in principle I am interested. If you give me your number, I'll check with her and get straight back to you.'

'OK Doug, but time is of the essence. Can you ring me by close of business today?'

'I'll ring you one way or the other by five o'clock. How's that?'

'Perfect. Bye for now.' He gave his direct number and the line went dead.

Doug wriggled around on his office chair, tilting up and down as it groaned in protest. He went through the possible questions in his mind. Surely he would set the agenda? So what did he want to be asked? How the centre came about, the need he had identified and sort to fill. The food bank. Moving from the despair of retirement coupled with bereavement, finding new horizons. All fairly safe stuff, talk about how his life had moved forward with unexpected events.

Did he want to mention injustice? Wally. Or religious intolerance?

No, not the time or place. Dangerous territory, could go anywhere. How long would he have? The odd occasion when he had time to watch morning TV told him interviews on *Debate UK* were about fifteen minutes in total.

Better ring his ghost writer and get her expert opinion. Her mobile went to answering machine. Damn. He rang Sally at the office. She thought it a good idea, with certain reservations. She echoed his concerns, once he was in the hot seat there would be no going back. He couldn't simply walk out, with thousands, probably tens of thousands, watching and listening. That would be embarrassing beyond belief. But if the agenda was set during a Zoom meeting, what more safeguards could he ask?

He needed caffeine to stimulate his brain into some kind of action. Decision time, to do or not to do. He walked round, from the kitchen to the lounge and back again. He ended up returning to the clickie room where Ruby was still asleep. She raised her head briefly when he creaked and dipped, then returned with a sigh to her gentle slumber.

The 'phone broke into his contemplation. Tracey. He explained the situation and his reservations. She was positive, saying go for it. Agree the questions, stick to the script, don't get side-tracked, be clear and concise. No rambling.

They'd get together when he had done the Zoom. She said she had to go, she was busy preparing an article for the next publication. All would be well.

All might not be well. He swung in his chair. Oh well, she's probably right.

His laptop was on emails and a message flashed up. A Zoom invitation tomorrow morning from Jane Atkinson.

Sally hugged him and wished him well for the Zoom meeting as she left for work. He hadn't used Zoom much but knew he had to click on the link to enter the meeting. As the time approached he clicked the link and adjusted the lid of his laptop so Jane could see him clearly on the built-in webcam. He tested the volume which was on maximum. Ruby watched all this with a bored expression. *Dad's talking to himself again, only this time to the bright light on that square thingie in front of him. Humans are such strange creatures.*

At five minutes to nine a figure appeared on the screen. He recognised Jane from the rare occasions he had seen her on television.

'Good morning Doug. Can you hear me OK?'

'Yes thanks. Can you hear me?'

'Loud and clear. It's good to meet you, if only virtually. I look forward to next Wednesday when we can talk face to face. You'll be going out from ten-forty-five, so I hope you can get to the studio latest seven-thirty for make-up, sound check etc. How's that sound?'

Like a very early start and a lot of faffing. He was rapidly going off the idea.

'Sounds OK. Long as I know what I'm supposed to be doing.'

'You'll be fine, Doug. I'll email you directions and what you need to know. Anything still not clear, send me an email and

I'll get straight back to you. Now then, what exactly would you like to talk about. You chat and I'll take notes.'

He quite liked her demeanour, friendly yet professional. He hesitated and she prompted him with a question.

'What do you hope will be the outcome of this interview?'

Outcome? Should there be an outcome?

'Well, I suppose to advertise the centre and food bank, show there is a need out there. I, eh, should there be an outcome?'

'Yes of course, you want to leave the audience with a broad opinion about your work and how it affects them. First, perhaps you could explain a little about your background, how it all started. I understand from your book that you had recently retired and were feeling lonely. You had just suffered the loss of your wife and were struggling. I'm sure those points will touch many viewers.'

Sounds reasonable.

'And you question your work as an Anglican vicar. Is that correct? This is a human interest story and people I'm sure would love to hear about your struggle and how it turned out positively, helping the less fortunate in society.'

The Anglican vicar bit alarmed him, that could lead into very muddy water, was open to various interpretations. He asked if that could be just mentioned but not explored. She agreed.

'You make me sound like a saint! I don't want to come over as all self-righteous, listen to me, I did it folks. That's not me at all.'

'I understand that, Doug. You simply tell your story and my job is the presentation to the audience. Does that make sense?'

Sort of. As long as you can be trusted. If it sounds too good to be true it probably isn't. Once bitten. Come on lad, you either say no now or get stuck in. What did he want? To give hope to those watching who could relate to what he was saying. To help them have a vision of a meaningful future, give them encouragement. He tried to explain this to Jane and she seemed to understand. He glanced at his watch and realised they had been chatting for over twenty minutes.

'OK, thanks Doug. I've got what I need. It's not so much asking you questions as allowing you to tell your amazing story. Look, I'm on air soon so I'd better say goodbye. If you have any questions or there is something you're not sure about, send me an email or ring me on my private mobile number. I'll put it in the email I'm sending this afternoon. And don't forget, we can iron out any final questions when we meet in the studio next week. Take care Doug, bye.'

He watched the message *End Meeting For All* appear on the screen, followed by *End*.

Chapter Seventeen

Doug set off for the television studio early the following Wednesday. Sally had seen him off with a big hug of encouragement, telling him to ring her as soon as he was on his way home. She would take Ruby to the office with her for the day.

As he drove, his mind shot backwards and forwards. He glanced with a smile at the pack of sandwiches and flask of coffee on the passenger seat Sally had given him. Comforting memories of home. He wished he was back there, safe and sound. He was going into the lion's den, but Daniel came out OK. Have faith lad, all will be well. You're not a ditherer, go for it! Sally and Tracey had told him it was a good idea, deep down he knew it could help viewers.

But live TV…

He parked the car and made his way to the studio building. At reception he was relieved to see his name on the list for that day and he was shown into the program's green room. Here were three other people waiting to be interviewed; a large middle-aged lady from a homeless charity, a young man who runs a homeless hostel and a strange looking lady in her thirties with dyed red hair and bright clothes. Apparently she is the leading light for a gay homeless charity.

As they chatted, it became clear to Doug that they each had a slot on that morning's program about homelessness. The batting order was the others first, with him bringing up the rear. The bright lady commented his was the best slot, as his interview would stick with viewers. She seemed to know what she was talking about, in fact they all seemed media regulars. Except him. He didn't know what to make of that, whether he just got lucky and this was the beginning of a media career. Oh yeah.

His concerned contemplation of this subject was broken by the appearance of their host. Jane looked ready for action, her make-up was perfect and her blue tailored suit with matching high heels complemented what Doug could see of the set through a window into the studio.

'Good morning. Welcome to the set of *Debate UK*.' Her manner was friendly, vibrant. She looked different from when he had seen her on the small screen, slightly older then her forty-six years and more care-worn. And smaller. He supposed studio lighting accounted for that, wondering what he would look like. Her perfectly coiffured auburn shoulder-length hair shone.

'Make-up will be along shortly. Now, any final points you want to discuss? We've all Zoomed and most of you know the score, have your scripts prepared.'

She looked from face to face. The others shook their heads confidently, they were clearly raring to go. Doug tried to ignore the sinking feeling in the pit of his stomach. Think of something happy; Sally, Ruby, anything.

Why did he feel even worse than being at the dentist? He wondered where the loos were in case he needed to throw up.

The others drank coffee or fruit juice and munched the treats, chatting ten to the dozen. Doug observed them in motionless silence. To be safe he asked the large lady sitting next to him where the loos were. Down the corridor, second door on the left.

Murmuring his thanks, he set off in that direction. Freedom. Should he keep on walking, surely this was the way he came in? The second door had a Gents sign on it. Bet she was right in everything, she seemed a know-it-all.

Wonder if she'll give me the winning weekend lottery numbers. Stop it, you're behaving like a child!

He leaned heavily on the washbasin and stared into the mirror. Make-up had better hurry up, his forehead was shining like a beacon and he looked a whiter shade of pale. The studio lighting would be much more intense, highlight every flaw. Worse still, his mind was blank. Focus man, focus. Breath deeply. Think what you're going to say.

He pulled out his wallet and stared at Sally's photo, smiling happily as she leaned against the Pilot's front nearside wing. They had chosen that emerald green dress together, he tried to remember where. Weird how the mind focuses on irrelevances at times of stress.

Better get back. He drew back his shoulders, took a deep breath and leaned towards the mirror.

'You Douglas are going to be great! You will shine! You are a star!' Partially convinced, he thought he'd better have a wee, then washed his hands, winking into the mirror as he rubbed his hands vigorously with a paper towel.

Back in the green room he was a new character. He talked, laughed, shared experiences, waved his coffee cup around to emphasise points. A make-up lady breezed in with her tray, expertly tended to the guests in order of appearance on the show and departed. Sally would burst out laughing if she could see him with black eyeliner!

The studio lights came up, instructions were shouted by the producer, Jane settled into her chair, last minute fussing by make-up, five second countdown and the show started.

An assistant led the large lady out of the green room and Doug watched in fascination as she appeared in the studio and sat opposite Jane. Jane was talking all the time as she introduced her guest. He could see on the screen in the green room that the camera did not pick up the large lady until she was seated opposite the host.

Doug was impressed with the interview, the large lady spoke well and put her case across with passion. In fact all three did. He lost count how many cups of coffee he had drunk, until a young lady assistant walked in with a clipboard and earphones, holding up four fingers.

'Four minutes Mr Spencer'.

His legs felt like jelly as he stood up and followed the assistant, his recent confidence had evaporated. He was told to stand at the side of the set and be ready to move to his seat when indicated.

The bright lady had gone and the camera was focused on

Jane who was wrapping up the last interview and preparing the way for Doug.

The seconds seemed like hours. The second hand on the huge studio clock ticked slowly. Point of no return Doug; nowhere to run, nowhere to hide. Prepare to be exposed before millions, naked, every word scrutinised, picked over, criticised. Truth will out. But will it? Or will it be obscured, deflected by clever journalistic interrogation? Family, friends, people who know him would either be watching live or see it on catch-up! Faces flashed across his mind. Would they feel they had to be kind, tell him he was great whilst hiding their true feeling? Feel sorry for him. Some might laugh behind his back. The millions of faceless strangers were one thing but people who know him… ouch. Right, enough's enough. Focus on the viewers who would receive comfort and strength from his words. Perhaps find inspiration to pull themselves together and look to the future.

The assistant whispered, 'You're on!' She led him to the chair, ensured he was in the correct position, smoothed a few out of place hairs that were sticking up, studied him from side to side, nodded and disappeared.

Someone held up a thumb and mouthed 'Action' to one of the many cameras.

He had been told to speak to the camera showing a red light.

Jane's cheery voice seemed to come from far away. He heard his name and a brief explanation of his background. Welcome Doug, then she asked him to tell the viewers how the centre came into being.

Off he went. Where the words came from was a mystery, later he wondered how he managed to say what he said with such confidence and sincerity. He started with finding himself retired and bereaved, lonely and confused. Then adopting Ruby, seeing the need to feed homeless people, the mobile catering van, the permanent building with a chapel, the food bank, the people he had met, using only first names.

He glanced at the clock, realising he had been talking non-stop for seven minutes. He looked at Jane. She was nodding and smiling.

'Thank you Doug, that was passionate and impressive. Can I ask you about feeling a failure as a vicar. I'm sure many of our viewers would like to hear more about that.'

Red light, not just on the camera. Steady lad, you suspected it was coming. Be careful. He spoke softly and thoughtfully about maintaining the status quo, not wanting to rock the boat. Perhaps being afraid to ask difficult questions about how the teachings of Jesus are especially relevant in our day. That people need to assess their faith, maybe make some changes. All within the firm grasp of church hierarchy. He was happy with his answer.

The next question was equally poignant. What were his thoughts on Muslims?

He replied that he accepted all religions; Judaism, Hindu, Buddhists, Islam, whatever. People are brought up in various religions and are mostly proud of their heritage. Some live according to their belief.

'But religion causes conflict, wars even. You can't deny that.'

'People cause wars. Humanity never has been and never will be, perfect. We have to learn to live together in love and forgiveness. Be compassionate and understanding.'

Realising he wasn't going to be drawn further, she terminated the interview.

The red light on the camera facing him went out, Jane's face dominated the screen as she thanked her guests, invited viewers not to miss the next *Debate UK* and signed off, reminding them they could contact the program via their website, email or Twitter. The studio lighting dimmed.

'Well Doug, that went well. What do you think?'

'Yes, it seemed to go OK. I take it you'll let me know any comments that come in, good or bad.'

'Sure. We'll email you all comments as they come in.'

He made for the door. Time to get home, tell Sally all about it.

∝

'A star is born!' was her first comment when he rang her from the car before setting off.

'Very funny. You haven't seen it yet.'

'No, but I will tonight, looking forward to it. Well done, you can relax now. Drive carefully. Love you.'

He put the 'phone back in his pocket and started the engine. Home Doug and don't spare the horsepower.

His mind went over the interview as he drove. Did it really go as well as he hoped it would? Yes, on balance. He didn't get badly ambushed which was a huge relief. No unexpected questions or snide comments. All good. He switched on the radio to his favourite music channel, tapping the wheel in time to the music.

∝

He heard the sound of her engine and the tyres on the gravel as she pulled in. At last, it wasn't as if he'd been waiting. He put the cottage pie in the oven and leaned casually against the worktop, arms crossed.

She dashed in with arms outstretched.

'Well done my darling, that's another string to your bow.'
They hugged.

'Don't speak too soon, could be a noose round my neck.'

She put the kettle on. 'Silly. Oh I can't wait!'

The 'phone rang. It was Tracey to congratulate him. They
chatted for a few minutes by which time Sally had made tea.
She called over her shoulder as she headed for the lounge.

'Just going to watch it, Tracey. Talk later.'

She switched on the television and digital box, settling down
expectantly. 'I hope you didn't forget to record it!' she called.

He came into the lounge carrying his mug. 'Oh sugar.'

'You didn't?'

'Do I look stupid?'

'No cos here it is.'

She settled into the sofa, mug in hand. Doug walked slowly
round the room, unsure whether he wanted to watch. She
patted the settee.

'Come on, sit down. I can't wait.'

They watched. Doug found it difficult looking at himself on
the screen. He peered forward trying to spot any imperfections.
He couldn't see any and he had to admit that it looked and
sounded pretty convincing.

Sally switched off with a big smile.

'Proud of you, Rev Doug. That will help so many people.
I wouldn't be at all surprised if you get lots of people wanting
to talk to you.' She kissed him.

'Or wanting to lynch me. But yes, it was OK, wasn't it. I
couldn't have done any better.'

They chatted until he suddenly jumped up, sniffing the air. Ruby was barking.

'The cottage pie's burning!'

He kept an eye on his incoming emails. He wasn't sure anyone would contact the program and less sure what they might have to say.

On Friday morning he saw an email in his Inbox. He paused, unsure if he wanted to open it. Inhaling deeply he clicked on the name *Debate UK*.

'Dear Doug, please find attached the comments received so far concerning your appearance on the show.'

He opened the attachment. Fourteen people had responded. Six wanted his email address or telephone number for advice. Three wanted to give a donation to his work at the centre. Two offered food for the food bank. But two stood out.

'You are a disgrace to your religion. You should be ashamed of yourself, you self-righteous prig. Why don't you become a Muslim, if they'll have you.'

He leaned back and the chair creaked more than usual as he swung nervously from side to side. OK OK, calm down. You're always going to get people who can't see beyond the end of their own nose. If you put yourself out there, you can't expect all hugs and kisses.

Criticism and misunderstanding go with the territory, it's the way of the media world. Two out of fourteen, that's a reasonable percentage. To distract his thoughts he tried mentally to work out the percentage.

Two over fourteen times one hundred. Irritated he pulled

out his mobile, clicking the figures into the calculator. Answer 14.2857143 percent. On the plus side, that meant 85.7142857 percent were positive. The figures never lie. I'm a fourteen plus percent failure or an eighty-six plus percent success, take your pick. Wow, the price of fame.

He made a mug of coffee and some toast. Ruby followed him round the kitchen hopefully. He sat at the table and fed her bits of toast, deep in thought. He should ring the people who wanted to talk to him. Members of the eighty-six whatever percent. But after he talked to them, they might tip over into the fourteen something percent. How would that affect the figures?

He put his plate in the sink and took his mug into the clickie room. Ruby followed, without hope of more food but she preferred to sleep on the carpet rather than the kitchen tiles.

He dialled the first name on the list. A Mr Davidson, no other details.

'Mr Davidson? Hello, it's Doug Spencer here. From the *Debate UK* show. I believe you want to talk with me?'

The line was silent for a few moments.

'Oh yes, that's right. Thank you for getting back to me so soon. Yes well, I think I am possessed.'

Doug almost dropped the mug he was raising to his lips. Possession! That was the absolute last thing he expected to hear. The voice sounded late middle-aged, calm, matter of fact. Over the years Doug had read about exorcisms and watched films like *The Exorcism of Mary Rose*, but his knowledge was very limited. Very.

As the man talked, Doug quickly typed *deliverance ministry* into Google. The following appeared:

In Christianity, ***deliverance ministry*** *refers to groups that perform practices and rituals to cleanse people of* demons *and evil spirits. This is done in order to address problems in their life deemed to be manifesting as a result of demonic presence, which have authority to oppress the person. Believers attribute people's physical,* psychological, *spiritual and* emotional prob-lems *to the activities of these evil spirits in their lives. Deliverance rituals are meant to cast out evil spirits, helping people overcome negative behaviours, feelings, and experiences. Each individual event is different, but many include some or all of these major steps: diagnosis, naming the demon, expulsion, and some form of action taken by the exorcised person after their exorcism to keep the demon from returning. The distinction between deliverance ministry and* exorcism *is that exorcism is conducted by priests given special permission from their church, while deliverance ministry is prayer for people who are distressed and wish to heal emotional wounds, including those purportedly caused by evil spirits. In both cases in casting out spirits, adherents believe they are following the example of* Jesus Christ *and his* disciples *given in the* New Testament. *The doctrines and practices of these ministries are not accepted by all Christians.*

Mr Davidson paused at the moment Doug finished reading the information on the screen. Doug had been listening whilst simultaneously trying to read. The stated problem was the man felt an evil spirit was controlling him.

'Well Mr Davidson, I must be honest and open with you. This really is an area in which I have no expertise whatsoever. Have you tried anyone else? Someone who is an expert in these matters.'

'Yes I have, but no-one understands or wants to help. You are my last hope.'

'I don't know what to suggest, I'm afraid. I'm sorry but I can't help you.'

Better to be up front in a case like this.

'Well, will you pray for me? Now.'

'Of course I will. And I will hold you in my prayers, Mr Davidson.'

Doug prayed, then he promised to ring him the following week. The man seemed to feel better and rang off with a 'Thank you for listening.'

Poor man. Perhaps he needs psychological help. Or that of someone who understands deliverance ministry. Or both. Doug felt uncomfortably helpless.

He looked at the other five names. No way could he face them right now, especially if their problems were anything like Mr Davidson's. Surely not. He went into the lounge, then decided he needed fresh air.

'Walkies.' As they walked, Doug pondered why a lot is talked about delivering us from evil but few understand what it means. Nor do they wish to. Evil's great triumph.

They walked for miles. When they returned to the cottage, Doug was thinking more clearly. People are people with problems few know or want to understand. Reside in a lonely darkness. Like him at the start of his journey.

He made a coffee and drank it as he leaned ruminating against the kitchen worktop. He made another and took it into the clickie room. He rang the numbers of the three who wanted to donate money to the centre and was impressed by their generosity. Two wanted to make monthly donations.

When he rang the two offering food to the food bank, he was blown away.

They were private supermarkets who promised weekly deliveries of non-perishable goods. Tins, cereals, toiletries, nappies and more.

By the time he rung the five remaining "Need to talk' people he was on a high. Even if they were like Mr Davidson, he felt he could cope. They were folk with family problems, three men and two women. Separation, pending divorce, the men expressing difficulty in maintaining contact with their children. None expressed any deep religious belief but felt he was a man they could talk to.

He concentrated on what they said, gave advice on issues within his remit.

Generally he was a listening ear; calm, soothing, a person who cared and genuinely wanted to help lighten their load. Two asked for prayer whilst on the line.

He told each caller they could ring him at any time and promised to ring them anyway the following week.

He stood up to stretch his legs. His back and shoulders were stiff and he swung his arms gently. Well, perhaps being on tele wasn't such a bad idea after all.

Oh, post, forgot to look at the post. He had picked up several letters from the hall floor earlier but the morning's events had overtaken him and he had thrown them onto his desk unopened. He flipped through them. Two for Sally, three for him. He put Sally's back on the desk and checked his post.

Bill, bill, hello I don't recognise this one. He picked up the letter-opener and slit open the thin brown official-looking envelope. It was from the centre landlord's solicitor.

Blah blah, what! Notice to quit! The landlord wanted to sell the property and was giving notice that the tenant must vacate the premises in three months.

He dashed to the filing cabinet and searched for the lease. As the rent is paid quarterly in advance, three months' notice must be given by either side.

That's mid June. He had done so much work and spent money converting the centre from a shop; built a kitchen, sorted the chapel. Oh no, where would he find such suitable premises again, pay for any necessary conversion? All in three months.

The office chair nearly collapsed as he crashed onto it, holding the letter loosely. Ruby sat bolt upright, realising something big and bad was going down.

The phone rang. Thelma was in labour and asking for him.

Chapter Eighteen

He threw himself into the car with Ruby close on his heels. Don't think about other problems, switch off. Concentrate on the matter in hand. Ring Sally. Right, do that when you get to the hospital.

It was fortunate he never used his mobile whilst driving as he suddenly noticed a bright light in his mirror. Sugar, speed camera. He glanced at the speedo. Thirty-nine. The day's getting better and better. He eased off the accelerator to thirty.

Arriving at the hospital he parked and rang Sally. Answering machine.

Wonderful. He left a quick message about Thelma and the hospital and dashed to the maternity ward. He was given a room number at reception after confirming his identity, was checked off on a list and hurried down the corridor.

He found Thelma's room and knocked on the door. It was opened by a gowned figure he assumed was a midwife, who looked at him questioningly over her mask. She nodded when he identified himself and indicated a basket by the door.

'Gown. Mask.'

When he was suitably attired she let him in and he saw two figures standing either side of the bed. Thelma was panting under the guidance of the midwife.

He had forgotten to switch off his mobile and got a glare when it rang. As he switched it off, he saw Sally's name on the screen.

He looked at the gowned man and woman on either side of the bed. The man came forward and shook his hand. He pulled down his mask slightly.

'Rob, Rob Thompson. You just be Doug. This is my wife Joanne.' He indicated across the bed. 'We're adopting Thelma's baby.'

Doug nodded to Joanne and waved at Thelma as he moved to Rob's side.

'Shouldn't be long now,' Rob commented excitedly. 'This will be our first.'

'Not the mother's first though,' observed the midwife in a flat voice. Thelma raised herself on the bed and looked at Doug.

'We had a baby girl a couple of years ago. She didn't make it, was only eight weeks. They said it was a cot death. Wally,' she broke down, 'Wally always wanted a girl. This one's a boy.' She sank onto the pillow.

Doug assimilated this information. He said a silent prayer. For Thelma, for Wally, for the baby they had lost, for this baby and his new life with Rob and Joanne. He felt angry and wanted to shout 'For the whole bloody world, for the forgotten and neglected, for the poor sods who live their lives in shit!'

He closed his eyes tightly in despair. Why does one pray with eyes closed, when everyone has to wallow in the crap they didn't create or deserve. Some do deserve it. Look at the crap, don't close your eyes. Pray wide-eyed to the God you believe in, He has to look at it all the time.

The day's emotion was getting to him, he was becoming irrational. He had to focus, for Thelma's sake. And Wally's.

They didn't have long to wait; a few pushes and out he came. Thelma turned away when asked if she wanted to hold him and the midwife gave him to Joanne. She showed him to Rob who gave Doug his mobile and asked him to take some photos.

Doug looked at the baby and thought he had Wally's features, certainly his nose. He said goodbye to Thelma with a smile, saying he would see her soon.

He wished luck to the new parents and with one last look at baby Thompson, left.

He rang Sally on his way to the car to give her the news, patted Ruby as he got in and they were on their way home. He kept well within the speed limit as he reflected on the day's events.

As he approached the driveway he saw Sally's car. She opened the door and hugged him so tightly it almost hurt. A wonderful, comforting hurt. They walked inside with their arms round each other. Ruby trotted alongside, sensing all was now well. Umm, good smells. Beef casserole.

As they ate Doug explained the day's episodes in chronological order. She stared at him in disbelief. When he had finished she stood behind his chair, putting her arms round him. Everything melted away until he thought about having to vacate the centre. That was a major headache.

The next morning Doug made calls. To anyone he could think of who might assist with finding new premises. There were more empty shops on the high street but nothing suitable. He couldn't work out how they could charge such high rents for such lousy premises. Why couldn't they just stay where they were? When everything is going well, why do you hit a brick wall? Get pulled down.

In desperation he looked at Ruby. 'Any bright ideas kidda?'

She lifted her head, gave him a sympathetic look and went back to sleep.

Great, fat lot of help you are!

The 'phone rang. Could it be a miracle, the solution to his dilemma? He drained his mug. Oh well, better see what's wanted. He lifted the receiver.

'Morning Doug. Ben Elliot here. Your appearance on *Debate UK* has been a big success, viewing stats are amazing. You really hit the right button with your comments. Look, we've just had a production meeting and we want you to head up a new Sunday morning program we're thinking about, *The Question of Religion*. It will go out every Sunday morning, be recorded on Fridays. We feel you're the man who could make this a success with your background. What do you think, interested?'

Host a Sunday morning television show? Come on, who's kidding who.

The possibilities and problems were enormous. Ben spoke again.

'Look, I know you want to think about it but believe me, this is a big opportunity. Think of all the viewers you could reach, open up so many avenues, get discussions going. And of course you'd be paid a fee and expenses. Tell you what, why don't you come to a meeting at the studio and we'll thrash out the detail. How's next Tuesday sound? Say eleven am. You won't be committing yourself but we can go through the proposed format and answer any questions you have. Yes?'

Nothing to lose getting more information, he thought. Anyway, he had more pressing things on his mind than television programs.

'OK, see you then.'

He replaced the receiver. Well well, that's a new one! He understood what a break this could be, how many people he could reach. Depending on how the network wanted to play it. In his imagination he saw *The Question of Religion* as a chance to open up a debate on different religions and their relationship to each other. Promote tolerance, understanding.

Who would contribute, who did the producer have in mind? Would Ben be the producer or someone else?

What were their thoughts? Would he have free reign or have to fit into a preconceived pattern?

Many questions. Oh well, wait and see. If he didn't feel right about it, he could say no. It could be a worthy challenge, using the airwaves to change entrenched, uneducated opinion. Bring harmony, bring people together. The possibilities were endless.

The anchor man of Alcatraz. Wow, wait til Sally hears about this one!

As he headed for the studio he felt good. He had run the idea past Sally, Tracey and his daughters with positive feedback. Go for it was the unanimous opinion. So here goes.

He was expected at reception and shown to a meeting room.

Ben welcomed him as people filed in. Plenty of coffee available on a table at the side of the room, even a plate of sandwiches. Good start.

He helped himself and sat at the long table. When people had joined them, Ben made introductions. They were all under forty, dressed in jeans and sweaters, except for a tall lady in her mid-thirties who was smartly dressed in jumper and skirt.

'Can I introduce you to Rhonda James, she will be your producer. I will be the exec.'

Ben went round the table, introducing the director, set designer and researcher. A production assistant took notes.

Doug shook hands with each one. As he sat down he looked at Rhonda. She seemed on the ball. Ben asked her to outline the program as she saw it, then they would put some flesh on the bones.

She explained that Doug's appearance on *Debate UK* had sparked the idea.

As she had watched it, she got the concept for a program which encouraged debate by a panel of experts and which would make viewers think about issues they may not have understood.

Doug was impressed with her and her professionalism. She obviously knew what she was talking about. He had a question.

'Can I ask please, do you have experience of this type of program?'

They all turned to him. Rhonda answered.

'Good question, Doug. I have produced several religious programs but nothing like this. You inspired me. Not the usual sweetness and light stuff but an open debate on important issues in our society. Not being afraid to dig under the carpet, shine a light on dark corners.'

'And Rhonda is an excellent producer, she has imagination and courage. To go where no woman has ever gone before.' Ben leaned forward.

'Doug, we want this to be a first, certainly where religion is concerned. A no holds barred scenario.'

'How much autonomy would I have? Would I be allowed to contribute within reason, both in the planning and the actual programs?'

'That's why you're here, Doug. The key to success will be in the debates that take place on screen, the way truth is both told and challenged. And in the creative planning,' Ben offered. He seemed very sincere.

Doug was surprised at himself. He felt quite at home here, like he had been involved in television for ages. Was that a good or bad sign? Was he getting too cocky with his newfound opportunities?

'You won't just be the front man Doug, you will be the centre, the person who makes the whole thing work,' Rhonda encouraged. 'The project will stand or fall with you, you will be the kingpin.'

There followed a technical discussion, led by the director. Possible set designs were floated, where the researcher should start looking. There would be a studio audience and demographics were explored.

After fifty minutes Ben finally turned to Doug.

'Well, you've heard the bare bones and some added flesh. Plenty more to flesh out but this is only an exploratory meeting, we'll have several before we get it right, ready to roll.' He paused. 'Are you up for it Doug? We need your agreement before we spend time and money on more resources. Are you the man for the job?'

All eyes focused on him again. Was he the man for the job? Hell yes, why not. Go for it.

'I'll certainly do my best. It all sounds very exciting.'

'Excellent! Thanks Doug, you won't regret it. Rhonda will be in touch soon to talk it all over and get the ball rolling.'

The meeting was over.

⊰

As he was walking to the car he rang Sally. She was delighted it went well, asked if she needed to call him *Sir* now. He replied *TV King* would do. She laughed, telling him to drive carefully and they would talk when they got home.

On the drive, Doug felt on top of the world. He gave Ruby half a sandwich from the meeting room. Good sandwich, fresh and tasty. She licked her lips in agreement.

He prattled away as Ruby sat watching him. No time to sleep, Dad is excited.

He talked himself through the meeting; the people he had met, the ideas mooted. The possibilities and the possible downsides. Had he gone nuts, was this reality, or was he biting off more than he could chew? Suddenly he was filled with doubt. He pushed them away, these people are professionals, they wouldn't have contacted him if they weren't confident he could deliver.

He saw a radar camera approaching and checked the speedo. All good.

⊰

He was in the clickie room waiting for Sally to return from work. He had so much to tell her. For some reason he wandered back to the beginning of his story, well not the beginning but the start of the main chapter. How the present was a stark contrast to the past. His mother flashed into his mind.

He had sat is this very room soon after he had moved in. No Ruby, no Sally, no future. Father Dougal had stared out of the cottage window on a frosty January morning. Opening the mobile catering unit for the first time and shouting at the sky 'Top of the world ma, top of the world!'

Top of the world. Jim had been such a large part of everything. Jim. Better ring him to put him in the picture. What would his reaction be?

'Hi Jim. Got some news to share with you.'

He explained about the possible TV program and how it came about. Ending with his doubt about being capable of meeting such a big challenge. He suggested Jim might like to be a member of the panel. When he finished, Jim said words he would always remember.

'Doug, everything you have done so far has been leading up to this. This is the pinnacle, the top of the mountain. Fly my friend, fly like the eagle. There is a huge congregation out there who need to hear what you and your panel have to say, to have their questions answered. I am always here if you want to offload, need to mull things over. And of course I will be praying for you. Thanks for the offer to be on the panel, but no. Look, I am a relic of your past, you must look to the future. New beginnings, new challenges.'

Doug felt a tear rolled down his cheek. What a man, what a pastor. A God-given gift. Jim said a wonderful prayer for him and the program.

∝

When Sally arrived home she approached his chair and put her arms round him. After a few moments in silence she said, 'Let's go into the lounge and you can tell me all about it.'

They snuggled on the sofa as he told her detail by detail. He left nothing out, including his call to Jim. She took it all in, then said softly: 'My darling, I am so proud of you.' She looked full into his face. 'And I have what I hope is good news as well.'

He stared into her eyes. Can there be more good news?

'I bought the centre this afternoon, or rather the building. Lock, stock and barrel. I knew the money from selling the bungalow would come in useful.'

Come in useful! He didn't know what to say. In the background of his mind he had been riding a fantastic high whilst being bugged by the notice to quit the centre. Did he really hear what he thought he just heard?

'I'm sorry, what did you just say?'

'I said I've bought the building, so you don't have to leave the centre. Ever.'

He was incredulous.

'I thought I was hearing things, angel voices. I don't know what to say.'

'How about dinner is served Madame, with a bottle of wine.'

Two days later, Rhonda James rang early in the morning. She sounded bright and breezy, ready to go. They had identified a panel and wanted a meeting as soon as possible for his approval.

A Roman Catholic priest, an evangelical pastor, a rabbi and a Muslim cleric. The rabbi is a woman. He would provide the Anglican, or ex Anglican, balance.

He wanted to tell her the joke about the priest, the minister and the rabbi who were on a boat in the middle of a lake:

The Priest says, 'I am really thirsty. I'm going to shore to get something to drink.' So he gets out of the boat walks across the water to shore, gets a soda, walks back across the water, and gets back in the boat.

The Minister says, 'I am also really thirsty. I'm going to shore and get something to drink.' So he gets out of the boat walks across the water to shore, gets a soda, walks back across the water, and gets back in the boat.

The Rabbi thinks to himself 'pretty cool. I will try it.' So he says, 'I am also thirsty. I'm going to shore and get something to drink.' He gets out of the boat and falls in the water and drowns.

Then the Minister says to the Priest, 'Do you think we should have told him where the rocks were?'

The Priest says 'Nah, It was the only way to get him baptized.'

He started laughing then checked himself, embarrassed. He asked if she had a date in mind. Next Monday at ten, in the same meeting room as last time.

As she rang off, she wondered if he was simply happy the program was taking shape or if he had finally lost it. She might have decided a bit of both if she had known the full story.

∝

Monday morning he was up bright and early, raring to go. He had told Sally about the delicious sandwiches provided so she didn't make any. How could she compete with the fodder given to television celebrities.

They kissed in the driveway and he was off. Arriving early with all traffic cameras successfully circumvented, he walked

Ruby round the car park. He reflected out loud on the words of Meister Eckhart, *'God is at home. It is we who have gone out for a walk.'* God is at home. But also here, always present. In the presence of Jesus. He wondered what the panel would be like. Would they have a sense of humour?

Humour had got him through so many difficulties in his life. If they were cold and stand-offish, assuming he approved them, he could always inject humour into the proceedings. Sometimes humour can lighten the load.

One reason people find change so difficult is because of the flawed belief that it's about finding the one thing that will make it happen. As if the challenge is in finding the right 'thing,' whether it's a tool, idea, or technique.

The truth is, human behaviour is a lot more complex than that. It's influenced by a highly complex set of changing conditions and factors. Making a positive change and making it stick is not about just one thing, but about the individual themselves, the people around them, and their physical environments.

He put Ruby in the car with the words, 'You didn't understand a word of that, did you kidda' and moved towards the building. You like a challenge, well this is going to be a biggie.

In reception he was given an identity card. Wow, things are moving he thought as he put it round his neck. Acceptance. A lanyard to hoist himself with, his very own petard. Goodbye Hamlet, come back another day. Focus man! Stop trying to deflect from decision-making, you're not normally like this.

He was the first to arrive in the room. He helped himself gratefully to coffee and a plate of sandwiches. Rhonda was next in. She gave him a rundown of the prospective panel as she poured coffee. They had been carefully chosen but the final decision was down to him.

The panel drifted in. First the priest, Father Tom. A jovial man in his late fifties with white hair and glasses, wearing a black suit and clerical collar. He gave the appearance of having been round the block a few times. Doug took to him straight away, he was a definite yes.

Next the rabbi, an attractive woman in her mid-forties dressed in a dark green suit. She kept tossing her long auburn hair every time she spoke.

The imam was next, a studious-looking man in his thirties with glasses and wearing a long black gown. He had a round kufi cap on his head.

Finally the pastor made an entrance, sweeping in like he owned the place. He looked like a businessman in his tailored suit and tie. He took a cup of coffee and sat down in silence. Doug took an instant dislike to him, there was something about his over confidence and the way he looked down his nose at people.

Doug was glad he was neither under-dressed nor over, in his tweed jacket and cord slacks. This was an interesting group. He was glad they didn't have a Mormon as coffee would be out of the question.

After ensuring they all had coffee and refreshments, Rhonda made introductions, leading into a conversation she hoped would assist Doug. She went through a list of questions she had on a clipboard.

How would they react to a studio audience who might ask difficult questions?

They were all confident they would cope. The pastor added

as far as he was concerned, silly comments would be summarily dealt with. Doug mentally ticked his list, 'Watch this person, could be trouble.'

How would they react if a fellow panel member expressed very different views from their own?

Each replied that they would be professional and supportive, explaining their point of view in a friendly atmosphere. Except the pastor who seemed a little unsure of the question, stating the answer depends on how radical the view being expressed is.

Doug made another mental note. In other words, if they differ from yours.

There were eight questions and Doug thought they answered sensibly and thoughtfully. Except the pastor, whose opinions stuck out like a sore thumb.

Need to talk to Rhonda about him.

The meeting ended with Rhonda thanking them for attending and saying she would be in touch again very soon. When they had departed she looked at Doug.

'Someone got up your nose, didn't they? He got up mine too.'

'Yes, far too cocksure of himself. The others seem fine. It isn't easy to bring a panel together with very different viewpoints, who will give and take, be gracious to each other's point of view.'

They were silent for a few moments. Then Doug leaned forward. Jim! He would make an excellent addition. True, he had not agreed when Doug mentioned it but he felt Jim did not want to steal his thunder, this was his show.

Doug was hopeful he could be persuaded. He mentioned the idea to Rhonda. She was in agreement, she trusted his judgement and anyway the couple of reserves she had on her list were doubtful.

'Give him a ring and see what he says. If he agrees, we can have another meeting next week. Then a trial run-through with the final panel to iron out any problems.'

Doug asked if they had a date for the start of the production. She replied that things were moving along nicely and the first Sunday in the following month was pencilled in. That would be a pilot, if viewing figures are acceptable it would continue the following Sunday.

He wondered what 'acceptable' meant. If the show was unsuccessful, then Goodnight Vienna.

As soon as he got home he rang Jim. Doug explained what happened at the meeting and that an opening had arisen. Jim was the man for the job as far as he was concerned. He had the experience and his stability and insight would be an asset to the program. When he had finished, Jim made a comment.

'You haven't heard of nepotism, I gather?'

'Oh come on Jim, I'm being completely impartial here. The right man for the right job, that's you.'

Jim thought for a few minutes. He did like the sound of the format and like Doug, he could see that many viewers could be reached, touched, inspired.

'OK, I'm in. As long as I get to sign more autographs than you.'

'Not funny Jim,' he replied, laughing as he rang off.

Chapter Nineteen

Time for reflection. Take stock, not quite in the dead of night but not far off.

Doug and Sally sat on the sofa in the lounge holding hands, balancing mugs of Horlicks. Ruby lay at their feet taking an interest in proceedings but feeling weary after another long day. They had just returned from the centre, the one they now owned.

Sally contemplated a lot during her working hours. About encouraging and supporting Doug, whilst trying to ensure he didn't take on too much. She worried that he was always busy and how this might affect his all-round health. But he couldn't be held back, he had to go where he felt called. She was relieved Jim was going to be part of the program, his support would be invaluable. A friendly face in what would be a mammoth and possibly unfriendly environment.

Thelma continued to attend the centre every evening, leading the choir. They had supported her as much as possible but she seemed to be coping with her independence and didn't want to talk much. She never mentioned the adoption, appeared to have accepted the inevitable and moved on.

Serena had moved to Manchester to be near Ashar and Basma. Officially she lived in a flat nearby but the authorities were aware they lived together most of the time. As long as she didn't mess up, start drinking heavily again, their future looked bright.

People come into one's life for a reason. She knew Doug had entered her life for a reason and would be eternally grateful.

Doug thought about Mary. How she would react to his present circumstances, a world which had opened up in ways they couldn't even have contemplated.

He was sure she would be happy, very content. Very proud. What a blessing to have that certainty.

Peter had raised Wally's injustice in the House of Commons during a session of *Question Time*. They take place for an hour every Monday to Thursday and his oral question was directed to the Lord Chancellor. The latter said he would look into the matter and agreed to meet with Peter soon to discuss it. Peter had said privately to Sally that he would press on until Wally's name was cleared, of which he was extremely hopeful.

Doug yawned and stood up to stretch his weary limbs. They had so little time these days to talk about things, it was all go and spending time together to reflect and catch up with each other was important.

'Time for bed, missus. Ready?'

'Ready boss. Sorry, I mean Mr Anchor Man.' She bowed mockingly.

Practice day. Doug had arranged to meet Jim in good time and they met in the studio car park. It was raining heavily as Jim ran to his car.

'Bad omen this Doug, maybe we should call it off,' he joked as he got in.

Doug told him to get in and cut the humour. He was on edge and needed to concentrate. Jim got the message and patted Ruby who had jumped onto the back seat. He whispered, 'Someone got out of bed on the wrong side this morning.' She wagged her tail vigorously in reply.

Doug stared out of the windscreen as the rain streamed down relentlessly. He couldn't see a thing, not with his eyes nor his mind. He looked at Jim with a frown of despair. This was the big moment, well not the big big moment because that was the opening program, but this was make or break time. If the panel didn't gel or answer questions fully and succinctly, there would be problems. He had some test questions prepared in his pocket. See what happens.

Jim understood his restlessness. He hadn't met the panel yet but realised what could go wrong. Egos could be the stumbling block; intransigence and stubbornness.

He took Doug's hand and closed his eyes. He felt the need for prayer as they entered the lion's den.

Doug thanked him when he had finished. They turned up their coat collars and made a dash for the entrance.

The building was becoming all too familiar. The receptionist waved at him as they entered and gave Jim a visitor's pass. Doug felt in his jacket for his permanent pass and hung it round his neck. All present and correct.

Rhonda had said the take would be in studio three where

the set was ready. As they entered he could make out a long news desk in the gloom with *The Question of Religion* blazoned across its entirety in yellow against a royal blue background. The wall behind was in pale blue and he could just make out white clouds drifting across.

Suddenly the studio was ablaze with light as Rhonda came in and he was able to fully appreciate the set. He introduced her to Jim. There were no camera crew or technicians as this was not a full rehearsal. The cameras stood motionless but seemed no less threatening. Their dull red eyes seemed to follow him round the set.

'Like it?' Rhonda asked.

'Yes, impressive. Who sits where?'

She explained that he would sit in the middle, with two panel members on either side. If he agreed, his friend Jim would sit on his left, with the rabbi next to him on the outside and the imam on the outside right with the priest directly on his right. He tried to picture this image as he studied the chairs from the rear. Seemed fine in his mind's eye, they could always change the positions if necessary. Might not be advisable to have two competitive thinkers sitting next to each other.

Speaking of which, in they filed. They had obviously been conferring in the green room, their joint appearance was too coincidental. Father Tom was still munching a sandwich with the explanation that he hadn't had time for breakfast. Doug smiled, he liked this guy.

Rhonda welcomed them and showed each to their seat. Jim was already in his. She walked slowly backwards as she surveyed the set. She looked at Doug who nodded as he took the middle chair. Taking the list from his inside pocket, he cut straight to the chase.

'Stephen Hawkin once said,

There is a fundamental difference between religion, which is based on authority, [and] science, which is based on observation and reason. Science will win because it works.

What does the panel think of that?'

'Not much,' commented the imam with a toss of the head.

'I like it,' said Father Tom, 'he's got a valid point.'

'Stephen Hawkin was a firm atheist,' interjected the rabbi. 'He spoke from a very entrenched position.'

Doug looked at Jim who remained silent. Come on Jim, you must have a point of view. Don't let me down.

The imam went into an intellectual diatribe about the authority of the Koran superseding any scientific authority. Science comes from man, man comes from Allah.

Father Tom yawned as he wiped crumbs from his lapel. The rabbi stared at the ceiling. Rhonda sat at the side of the set, writing on a clipboard.

Doug despaired. Should he go on to his next question? He was about to move on when Jim spoke.

'Imagine you are a homeless person, living on the street. Life has treated you badly. Religion is low on your list of priorities. Yet Doug and me know such people who have survived and found time for religion. Not from observation or reason but personal experience.'

Doug wanted to applaud. Father Tom did. For Doug, religion is about experience, personal belief. Authority is one thing, experience quite another. No-one has the right to tell you what to believe, you either do or you don't. End of.

It's taking shape, we'll get there. He had a good grasp of the panel's personalities; he could handle them, bring out the best. Maybe he should be more proactive, give a lead? He introduced two more questions, chaired the debate without favour, then called it a morning.

When the studio was empty, Doug and Rhonda went into a huddle. Jim examined the set.

Rhonda explained that researchers were looking for their first audience, anyone could apply. Their questions would be collected beforehand, Doug would know what they were but not the panel. He would ask each questioner to ask their question in a prepared order, then ask the panel to respond whilst taking comments from the audience. A successful tried and tested format.

The rain had ceased as they walked to their cars. Doug suggested they go to a café for a chat. They were awash with coffee but there were alternatives. Fish and chips were agreed, with mushy peas, tea and bread and butter. Ruby jumped out of Doug's car in expectation as soon as he opened the door.

They enjoyed their meal, as did Ruby as she chewed pieces of fish and a few chips. They discussed the trial broadcast from every angle. Jim was positive, saying it had real possibilities. The panel were a diverse bunch who needed encouragement and control, but no major problems. Stroke their egos and reap the reward.

Doug was grateful for Jim's input. He too saw positives but was perhaps too close to see clearly, he needed to take a break and look at the wood without the trees. He smiled as he thought of Father Tom, he was a tree trunk who could lighten discussions and bring some humour. He was already developing a plan to use the good priest positively in the program. It was clear where the imam stood but the rabbi was as yet an unknown quantity.

They agreed to keep in touch and returned to their cars. As they shook hands, Jim asked him to give Sally his love.

The first recording went well. Doug felt at home in front of the cameras and soon got used to the bright studio lighting. He kept his gaze on the camera with a red light and brought in each member of the panel and the audience as questions were asked and answered. It had been decided how many questions could fit into an hour and he kept an eye on the large studio clock.

He felt in control with his friendly, reassuring voice and grasp of the issues raised. The rabbi surprised him with her insight. When the imam made a debatable comment in answer to a question about women and Islam, she brought up the Taliban and the role of women in a free society.

She also mentioned the ordination of women in the Catholic Church, which caught Father Tom on the back foot as the audience applauded. He responded by stating that he fully supports the ordination of women to the priesthood, surprising the panel and no doubt his bishop.

Suddenly the hour was over and Doug got the signal to wind up. The camera focused on the panel began to fade. Closing music came up, the credits rolled and the lights dimmed. As workers crowded onto the set, Rhonda gave him a thumbs up with a smile, then put her thumb and little finger to her ear mouthing, 'Call you later.'

Sunday morning. Doug and Sally sat down in the lounge just before viewing time. The mantle clock ticked forward slowly towards eleven am. Doug nervously fingered his mug. Sally was relaxed and excited. She switched on.

The credits for the previous program rolled up the screen. A female voice sweetly announced *The Question of Religion,* music came up and the picture zoomed in on Doug's upper body as he sat in the centre of the panel. Sally jumped up and down on the sofa, clapping as his voice welcomed viewers and introduced the panel. Doug felt queasy.

It was over and the credits rolled. He stood up, switched off and looked at her. What did he expect? Praise, criticism, sympathy? She simply stared at him in wonder.

'Have I told you lately that I love you, Anchor Man?' She stood up and hugged him. 'Well I do. Very much.'

As they kissed, Doug's mind flashed back to when he had opened the mobile catering van for the first time. She started as he broke free and shouted at the ceiling, 'Top of the world ma, top of the world!'

Ruby barked in appreciation.

THE END

By the same author

Sacred Memoirs of a Retired Failure
ISBN 978-1-915494-14-6

As this remarkable book, *Sacred Memoirs of a Retired Failure*, shows both in an entertaining and enlightened way, retirement is a life challenge in itself. The busy hub of life is ended and there is time to evaluate. If recent bereavement is added to the equation, contemplating the future may be almost unbearable.

Doug is in this situation. He struggles with loneliness as he moves into a new home, tries to make some sense of his past and find a future. He is haunted by feelings of failure in his career as an Anglican clergyman. He dearly misses his wife Mary and her support; he knows that it is only she who could have made sense of his constant questions and doubt. Before Mary died, Doug promised her he would write a book in retirement, a sort of autobiography.

He rescues Ruby, an abandoned dog and feels less lonely. Then he meets a lady of whom he has high hopes, but she lets him down. In his search he finds a challenging, exciting option which, Doug hopes, will join the pieces of his life together.

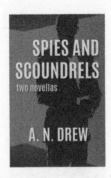

Spies and Scoundrels - two novellas
ISBN 978-1-915494-25-2

This fascinating and remarkable book, *Spies and Scoundrels*, consists of two highly imaginative novellas. The first, *Time to Say Goodbye*, explores how England might look in 2026. Post pandemic with many unresolved problems remaining, Government finances are dire and the country is directionless and unstable. People have gone into voluntary lockdown to avoid the violence on the streets. The scene is set for a change of Government, with a radical plan. A scapegoat group in society is identified and vilified. History does indeed repeat itself.

Death's Final Wicket is a spy thriller set in London, Oslo, Buenos Aires and Jerusalem. Bible Codes in the Torah (first five chapters of the Old Testament), supposedly point to various modern day events such as Hitler, Yasser Arafat and a nuclear war emanating from North Korea. Governments interpret these codes for their own ends. Meanwhile, a new terrorist organization, with its own plan, complicates matters. British Intelligence has the man with the right background to sort through the competing issues.